FIRE AT WILL'S

AN ESTELA NOGALES MYSTERY

CHERIE O'BOYLE

Printed in the United States of America

****

O'Boyle, Cherie
        Fire at Will's/written by Cherie O'Boyle
        ISBN   978-0 997 2028 5 4

Library of Congress Control Number
2014908643

2014, Cover by Karen A. Phillips, www.PhillipsCovers.com
Author photo by Nick Van Wiggeren
Author photo edit by Donald Goodenow

DEDICATION This story is for all who wait for me at the Rainbow Bridge: Deedle, Amigo, Chiquita, Sonny, Puff, Tammy, Max, Mickey, Rogan, Poppy, Delilah, Sampson, Kipp, Thibodeax and Scout♡

THANK YOU! In many ways, the story of how this book came to be is similar to how the mystery is solved: with much collaboration. It is with deep appreciation that I acknowledge the contributions, encouragement and support of my friends and advisors, Petey Connolly, Consuelo Baratta, and Marilyn Reynolds. Grateful appreciation also to Barbara Hayes, Ann Page, Nancy Loes, Wendy Smith, Joan Lacktis, and Maureen Blair, for their generous assistance.

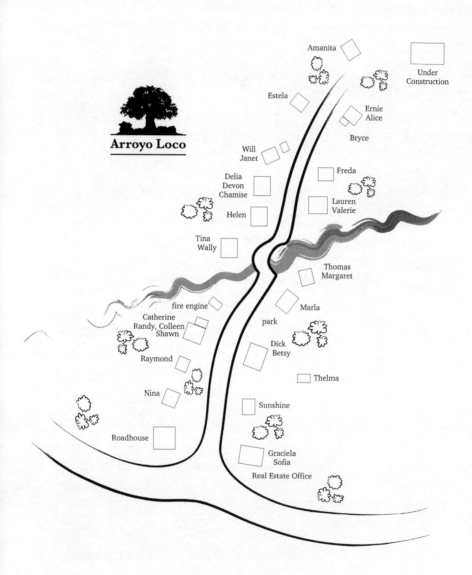

Arroyo Loco

Amanita

Under
Construction

Estela

Ernie
Alice

Bryce

Will
Janet

Freda

Delia
Devon
Chamise

Lauren
Valerie

Helen

Tina
Wally

Thomas
Margaret

fire engine

Marla

Catherine
Randy, Colleen
Shawn

park

Raymond

Dick
Betsy

Nina

Thelma

Sunshine

Roadhouse

Graciela
Sofia

Real Estate Office

CHAPTER ONE

It's a good thing the fire at Will's house started when it did. A half an hour earlier the residents of Arroyo Loco were still glued to their television screens, absorbed in the season finale of American Talent. Half an hour later, most would have been sound asleep. Left alone, the voracious fire would have consumed all of Will's house along with its gruesome contents. From there, the flames may have continued up the narrow flue of the oak and scrub brush canyon to my own house, nestled snugly under a spreading madrone. Nothing but ashes would have been left from which to glean clues as to what, or who, ignited that fire.

Records show the alarm was called in by Freda von Liesing, from her home directly across the road from the Rosenblums' at 9:21 p.m. Pacific Daylight Time. Twenty-one minutes to maneuver her plump, garishly caftan-clad figure out of the maroon recliner, visit the facilities in her vintage '50s pink- and blue-tiled bathroom, then head to her kitchen for a slice of left-over apple strudel. According to Freda's report, it was then that the fire at Will's, reflecting on the kitchen window, caught her eye. White-hot flames were snaking out the second story windows, pushing black smoke billowing above. The crackling was so loud she could hear it from inside her own kitchen.

No one questioned Freda's account. Even if someone had, no one would have blamed her for taking a few extra minutes to consider her course of action. Ever since their arrival in Arroyo Loco a year or so ago, Wilhelm Rosenblum and his wife, Janet, have been among the most challenging of neighbors.

This is not to suggest there is any shortage of hard-to-get-along-with neighbors residing along the narrow asphalt lane that winds through Arroyo Loco. Amanita Warten, chair and only voting member of the Arroyo Loco Homeowners Association Landscaping Committee, is an excellent example of a difficult neighbor, and one with whom Will Rosenblum is in near-constant conflict. Amanita adamantly requires that permission be granted before planting anything, anywhere, including a bit of lawn or seasonal vegetables like zucchini. Planting even in the area behind one's house is scrutinized. What's more, she rarely grants permission for anything that is, in her opinion, invasive or non-drought-tolerant. Zucchini, for example, is not allowed because, as anyone who has ever planted a zucchini knows, they can be quite invasive, at least for a season. As a rule, trying to make decisions jointly about our land and the houses constructed on it creates seemingly endless opportunities for conflicts, confusion, and confrontations between neighbors in Arroyo Loco.

Ours is a small village of about twenty mostly older, somewhat weathered houses located in the coastal mountains of California, about half an hour inland by a two-lane winding highway from the beaches of Morro Bay. The rolling golden hills around us are cattle range land, trending toward vineyards. A few ranch hands settled their families along this bucolic canyon in the early 1930s. They named their community Arroyo Lobo, Spanish for Wolf Canyon. Unfortunately, a typo down at the county courthouse when the deed for our association was recorded changed that to Arroyo Loco, Crazy Canyon, and that was the moniker that stuck.

On that rainy Friday night in October, Freda's phone call triggered an ear-splitting siren from the alarm mounted on the garage where our secondhand fire engine is housed. I know it was ear-splitting because my two border collies and I were standing about 50 feet down canyon. My name is Estela Nogales. Slightly shorter than average, I keep my curly dark hair short to avoid looking like an unkempt poodle. I prefer to think of my body-type as sturdy or strong, rather than soft and puffy, although others may disagree. An internet dating site might describe me as cute. This should not be taken to mean I have ever been on an internet dating site. Single now—I have been there, done that, and already worn out the T shirt. Overworked but underpaid, I am a clinical psychologist in the student counseling center at the university fifteen miles south of home.

When that fire alarm went off, my older border collie, Scout, lifted his nose, stretched his neck out, and let loose with a howl that almost matched the fire alarm in its piercing shrillness. Throughout the rest of Arroyo Loco the wailing siren was met, for the most part, with a lot of grumbling from folks already half ready for bed. It had gone off three times recently, all false alarms triggered by somebody dialing a wrong number or kids playing with the phone. The alarm before that was set off by an actual fire in the community kitchen during a potluck. That fire was extinguished by an alert high school kid with a wet dishtowel. It was out before the volunteer firefighters had a chance to get their jackets on.

The kitchen was originally built many decades ago as part of a highway roadhouse. Beer and barbecued ribs were served there, and live music was featured on Sunday afternoons. Now we use the old single-story building as a meeting hall and community kitchen. We put plastic tablecloths on the grease-stained tables for our potlucks. On Saturday mornings some folks drag a few of the broken-down chairs out to the wide porch for coffee and a bit of gossip. Twice in election years the building serves as the local polling place. Mail boxes are mounted under the porch overhang so the mail carrier doesn't have to trek up the canyon road to deliver. The mobile library truck used to stop there on Wednesdays until it broke down. There was no money in the county budget to repair it, so that was the end of that.

Across from the roadhouse, I watched as the door burst open. Three men much past their prime tumbled out and took off up the canyon road. They had been sitting, as they usually did on a Friday night, at the bar along the back wall sharing a bottle. Our hamlet does not generate much excitement, so the occasional fire alarm is greeted in the bar with a fair amount of stumbling off stools and bumping into one another. This night, Thomas Knapp emerged first, still clad in his bedroom slippers. He veered off toward the house he shared with his mother, probably to put on his boots. Wally Smutts hollered that he too needed something from home, but Wally's aversion to anything resembling work is all too well known. His skinny rear-end sprinting up canyon was the last anyone saw of him that night. Only Ernie Bantam hitched his pants up over his ample belly, slicked back what was left of his hair, and trotted off in the direction of the fire engine garage.

As I watched them run, a faint glow up canyon caught my eye. Two thoughts in quick succession. First, maybe this time the siren wasn't a false alarm. Second, and more horrifying, my house was up in that direction. Our homes are strung out along the curves of the canyon road, close enough together so that all residents have good views of at least two or three other houses. This is a great place for busy-bodies and snoops to live because almost everyone can see all the neighborhood comings and goings. From down by the roadhouse, I couldn't see around the curves to where this fire might be burning, but it was definitely in the direction of my house.

I dashed across the street onto Nina's porch, dragging the dogs behind. Peering into her brightly lit dining room, I could see Nina Arriaga working intently on one of her interior design projects. I tapped on the glass, then tapped harder, trying to quell my fears. That glow in the sky had me worried. She lifted her head, her dark eyes trying to penetrate the blackness outside. Diminutive, she moved like a graceful dancer with perfect posture as she rose, came to the door, and flipped on her porch light.

"*Hola, chica.*" She tipped her head in the direction of the siren. "*¿Que onda?*" Swinging the door wider, she invited me inside. The soft lighting in her stylish living room spoke of exquisite taste. Although we don't know each other as well as I might like, Nina is probably my closest friend in Arroyo Loco. She's a professional decorator, and I'm always curious to see the latest additions to her artfully designed home. But not tonight. That siren was still wailing, commanding serious attention.

"*No se´*, I don't know, but it looks like there might really be a fire up there. Can we take your car to go see? Please?"

5

In the daylight a person can walk the whole length of the canyon in about fifteen minutes, but at night it can be treacherous, especially with the old and rarely driven fire engine racing up the road, which it soon would be, I hoped.

Nina lifted keys and a raincoat from their hooks beside the door. She slipped into her clogs. "Okay," she agreed. "Only for a minute. I have this job to finish. I'm sure it's nothing, Estela." We climbed into her sleek silver Lexus with the leather interior, my dogs hopping eagerly into the rear seat. I saw Nina glance back, quickly managing to control her horror. Shiner, the younger dog, let his ears drop down and softened his brown eyes in a warm smile. He stretched his head between the seats, gave Nina a friendly nuzzle on her cheek, then quickly retreated as though he knew his gesture might not be entirely appreciated. I handed her a clean hanky.

As we drove past the fire engine garage, the volunteer fire chief, Dick Carper, and Ernie appeared to be having trouble getting it unlocked. They were, as usual, arguing with each other. Raymond Watts, the Homeowners Association President, was coming up behind them. A big man, he turned and waved. His chocolate brown skin with grizzled graying hair always reminded me of a giant double-fudge brownie with powdered sugar frosting. Nina's car crossed the rickety bridge and rounded the bend. Like a huge bonfire, the flames consuming Will's house exploded upward in front of us. We sat stunned. The ridge line behind the house glowed orange against the clouded night sky. Shadows of the oaks jumped, dancing crazily on the bright background.

"Oh my god, Estela! Will's house is on fire! *Dios mio!*" Nina wrenched the wheel, pulling the car hard into the adjacent driveway, narrowly missing Helen, who was running across the blacktop from her house on the other side of the road. Her head was turned, her eyes fixed on the flames. I don't think she saw us at all. Nina and I leapt from the car, then stood, watching in awe. Even from this far away the flames turned our cheeks a hot rosy-brown. After the initial shock, I felt relief that the fire appeared to be confined to Will and Janet Rosenblums' house. Then I flashed a moment of survivor's guilt. Only after that did I realize how much danger still threatened my own home. One puff of an up-canyon draft generated by the fire itself could easily explode into that copse of oaks behind Will's house. From there it would roar all the way up the canyon and beyond. Wildfires tear through California's coastal hills every year, taking homes, livelihoods, and lives with them. With the addition of wind, spheres of pure fire could grow larger than a house, jump four lane highways, and take off again on the other side. I'd seen it happen myself.

"*Dios mio*, Estela. Your house is next." Nina breathed next to me, still transfixed by the flames. As the fire consumed Will's house, it seemed inevitable that it would continue to rage through the rest of the canyon. All I could think about was stopping the flames now. Leaving the dogs secured in the rear of the car, we rushed to help neighbors who were gathering hoses in Freda's front yard. With only Freda's dim porch bulb and the light from the fire to guide us, we connected three hoses and hauled them across the road. Not long enough.

Appearing from behind Freda's house, Bryce arrived dragging another long hose. As usual, he was whining. "Why do you have all these hoses, Freda? Amanita and I put in a drip line for your plants. You don't need all these hoses! We agreed to go with drip lines instead!"

Although no one else paid him much attention, by the time we finally got the hoses laid out I was ready to use them to strangle Bryce. Even on the rare occasions when I agree with him, that whiny tone in his voice just sets my teeth on edge. Somewhere in his late twenties, Bryce still lives in his parents' converted garage, still dresses in the striped tee shirts his mother buys for him, and still sports the same little boy hair-cut he's worn since he was about eight years old.

After we yanked and rerouted the hoses, Freda was finally able to crank the water on full. Holding onto the end of a hose turned on full blast is not that easy. It took two of us to get it aimed in the right direction. Every time we got close enough to do any good, the heat of the fire drove us away. We did get the porch roof soaked, along with a couple of innocent bystanders. For a while we managed to keep the front wall of the house standing. The whole enterprise held a certain degree of irony, because the hoses would not have been where they were if Will himself had not used them to drown Freda's magnolia tree.

Will was one of those residents who insisted that everything planted in Arroyo Loco must be drought-tolerant. It was his opinion that because magnolias need regular irrigation they should not be permitted in our oak canyon. He argued bitterly with Freda until she planted the magnolia anyway. Then, in his usual passive-aggressive mode, he watered the poor tree to death when it was but a few months old.

Although they can't always name it, most people are familiar with passive-aggressive behavior. When someone agrees to go along with the plan, then, in complete innocence, sabotages the whole enterprise, that's passive-aggression. And that's our Will. When an idea he doesn't support is implemented in spite of his protest, he waters it to death.

Speaking of Will, I looked around for his lanky figure. He wasn't among those of us struggling with the hoses. Several other neighbors stood watching the fire from under the skeletal remains of the magnolia tree. He and Janet must be with them. We started to drag the hoses toward the rear of the house where the flames were more intense, but Thomas, arriving ahead of the fire engine, drove his truck across our makeshift hose, squashing one of the brass connections.

In all fairness to the volunteer firefighters, they did the best they could under the circumstances. They got the fire engine started, drove it up to the scene, and backed it around so the headlights would illuminate the now mostly burned up house. After a brief altercation with Dick about who knew best how to fix it, Ernie got the pump going. It was really no one's fault that a tiny leak had apparently drained at least half the water out of the tank by the time Ernie got the pump started up. That old fire engine sits in its dilapidated garage for weeks at a time between alarms, so it was no wonder the leak wasn't noticed before. Even when the pump got to working and the hose was aimed in the right direction, the thin stream wasn't much stronger than what we had been getting out of our garden hose arrangement.

There was quite a crowd huddled in Freda's small front yard by then. With relief, I let the fire fighters take over and joined the rest of the neighbors there. Lauren, from next door, stood next to me. She's a tiny woman in her 40s, dressed as usual that night in worn jeans, a flannel shirt, and moccasin slippers. Helen, at about the same age, towered over Lauren. Helen is not fat. She's one of those "big-boned gals" who make the rest of us feel like midgets. There were others there. The young mother who rarely comes out of her house except to go to work was there, holding a silent and wide-eyed toddler wrapped in a pale blue baby blanket. There are only a few children in Arroyo Loco, maybe six or seven. Like most of their elders, they are rarely seen outdoors. On this scary night, the toddler peered warily out from his makeshift hood, not uttering a sound.

Dick Carper's diminutive wife, Betsy, along with their next door neighbor, a woman who calls herself Sunshine Rainbow, had hitched rides on the engine, certainly in violation of some regulation forgotten in all the excitement. They joined us, both wrapped in long fuzzy bathrobes. Sunshine's flashed bright multi-colors in the dim light.

Conspicuously missing from the group in Freda's front yard were Will's closest neighbors. That seemed odd. No car in their driveway, no lights in their house. Were they lurking inside, peering out as the fire destroyed the Rosenblums' next door? More curious, where were Will and Janet? They could be anywhere in the shadows around the house. There were a couple of figures closer to the garage, and maybe that was someone in the white wicker chair on Freda's front porch.

As the firefighters worked, the rest of us moved away, watching. Nina curled her hand in front of her mouth. She leaned in to my ear. "Don't you think it's suspicious that his house catches on fire a couple of weeks after Will tried to burn down the Carpers' fence?"

My eyebrows shot up, and I turned to her. "Oh, you're right! I forgot about that!" Will read in a gardening magazine about using a special torch made to burn weeds, and about two weeks ago he'd decided to give it a try. Not wanting to spend the $49.95 to buy the garden torch, he figured his old welding torch would work equally as well. So he put himself in charge of clearing the star thistle growing along Dick's wooden fence. That Saturday morning he got out there and promptly set the fence ablaze. Burned about half of it down, too, before his yells and the smoke brought Dick outside to douse it.

"Really," Nina mumbled behind her hand. "Do you think Dick might have something to do with this fire?"

Betsy, a fiercely loyal wife, and a woman apparently with uncommonly good hearing, indignantly rebutted. "Dick had nothing to do with this fire! Can't you see him there risking his life to put it out?" She waved in that direction. A few of us looked across the road where Dick was still holding the end of the now-deflated firehose with a thin dribble arcing a couple of feet in front of him. He did not look so much like a man risking his life as he did a man finishing up a good pee.

Nina raised an interesting question though. How did this fire start? Was it Dick taking revenge? Or could it have been Will fooling around with his torch again?

In the end, it was Mother Nature who took pity on our little town. She fatally drowned the fire with a heavy downpour shortly before the trickle from the fire engine's depleted tank gave out entirely. What was left of the house and its contents sizzled, smoked, then began to emit the acrid stench of wet ash. Outfitted in dirty yellow rubber jackets and fire hats, smelling of tired old men, Dick and Ernie stood with the rest of us by Freda's dead magnolia watching the rain finish off the last of the smoking embers. As we stood in shocked silence, part of the second story roof caved in, briefly revealing pink roses on the wallpaper of a bedroom, before it too crumpled and fell.

In the quiet that followed, someone whimpered. A few "oh my gods" and similar references to deities were whispered. Soft moans could be heard as folks comforted one another. My emotions were mixed. The loss of the Rosenblums' house was shocking and sad, but it did appear, at least for the moment, that my house had escaped a similar fiery fate.

"Dick didn't start this fire," Sunshine, our resident psychic, intoned firmly. "The universe caused this fire to manifest in Will's life because of his suspicious expectations and thoughtless actions. Too many people in this community directed negative energy toward Will. That is what ignited these flames."

I like Sunshine, I really do. Sometimes she's like a sister to me. Her aging hippie persona, her usual flowing tie-dyed attire, the wafting fragrance of patchouli, even her chakra headband. For me it generates a fond nostalgia for days gone by. At other times it's as though a hot air balloon has swooped down and she's hopped on board for a ride. She was soaring now. Usually, I can take her pronouncements with whatever germ of truth may be hidden in them. It was a little harder tonight, and not only because of her giant Mickey Mouse bedroom slippers.

Arroyo Loco does include in its population more than a fair share of wing nuts who believe, nearly all evidence to the contrary, that wishing hard enough will cause dreams to come true. They firmly believe that focused attention is all that is required to make one's most cherished desires real, including wealth, perfect health, and apparently the burning down of an enemy's house. What happens when one person's dream conflicts directly with another's, I am not wise enough to know. Presumably, whichever one brings more focused positive attention to the task wins. For me, I come from more skeptical stock and am yet to be persuaded. My sainted Irish mother, may she rest in peace, always said, "Wish in one hand and spit in the other. You'll see which one fills up first," which pretty much sums up my thoughts on the subject.

The downpour settled into a steady drumming of rain. A few murmurs started about going home. Thomas bundled a couple of folks into his truck for the ride down canyon. He climbed into the driver's seat, backed and filled until he got the truck turned around on the narrow road, then drove squarely across our hose connection again, flattening it irretrievably. A few others pulled rain hats lower and drifted away.

Still feeling anxious about the possibility of the fire continuing further up the canyon in the thick underbrush, I searched the figures moving in the darkness for Raymond. We locked eyes. He was also searching the crowd. His brow furrowed. "Hey," he called out to no one in particular. "Does anybody know where the heck Will and Janet are tonight?"

Good question. There was some mumbling as people wondered aloud and the question was repeated to those who missed it. Bryce called that he'd seen Will over by Delia's. Betsy said she was sure Janet went into Freda's house, and Lauren went in to check. We all glanced around in the shadows. Lauren came out shaking her head. It appeared no one knew the whereabouts of Will and Janet. For a charged moment of silence, we considered the possibilities. There had been fires before in our dry canyon, but no one had ever died in a fire here. If the Rosenblums were at home when this fire started, where were they now?

Helen called out, her voice ringing over our heads, "Is his car in the garage?"

Good thinking. Simultaneously Dick and Ernie broke toward the small freestanding garage, racing each other the 40 feet to the door. The rest of us stumbled along after them in the dark. If Will's 1994 silver Honda with the dented left fender was not in there, we could have some assurance that Will and Janet were away. If the car was in the garage, well, nobody wanted to think about what that might mean. I shot Nina a horrified glance. She had both hands over her mouth.

The garage door was secured with at least three serious looking padlocks fastened onto heavy duty hasps. Wonder what Will was keeping in there that required that level of protection? Stumped, we stared at the ancient board-and-batten garage. Then fourteen-year-old Randy appeared, Arroyo Loco's most recently convicted juvenile offender. Clearly not for the first time, he lifted a loose board sideways, revealing the right fender and tire of a silver sedan. The car was home and so, most likely, were the Rosenblums. It may have been my imagination, but as he gazed in at the car, Randy looked startled and a little sick. By now, the smoke from the fire had settled in low over the canyon, reflecting the fire engine headlights. We probably all looked slightly greenish as we peered inside.

Raymond, who always knows on whose shoulders the chips will eventually fall, stepped back slowly, looking again at the house. After gazing bleakly for a few moments at the dripping wreckage, he secured the chin strap on his hat, flipped on his headlamp, and trudged off toward the front porch of the ruined house. We all moved around the garage to watch. Raymond gingerly climbed the stairs. Testing his footing with each step, he eased inside the darkened doorway. At first, we could hear him shuffling around inside with the occasional whack of his axe as he cleared debris. Then he was gone in silence for what seemed like a long time. When he reappeared and leaned his shoulder against the jamb, it was hard to see his face. He was covered with ash. His oversized jacket had lost its color and sheen. Slowly, he came toward those of us who remained, watching. His face was an unreadable blank.

"Are they...are they in there...?" Ernie swallowed hard.

Raymond looked slowly around, sweat streaking his dark face with white ash. The group shifted, folks trying to see his expression in the shadows of the reflected light. He wiped his hand slowly down his face, then looked at the ground. "I dunno," he replied, his deep voice rumbling in the darkness. He stared at his booted feet. "I can't tell. But something's not right. It's too dark, too smoky. Everything's a mess. I can't tell what's in there. I couldn't get in very far. I didn't want to disturb any... anything. Something's not right."

Stunned, no one spoke. Nearly every one of us standing there had engaged in some kind of serious altercation with Will during the past few months. Most of us wished we could vote him off the island, so to speak, but had something really awful happened to him? This was hard to contemplate. We stood there in horror, shooting guilty glances at one another, not breathing. Several of the women in the group pulled closer together. With a trembling voice, Nina quietly asked, "Did you see anything of Janet?"

"I'm sorry," Raymond answered. "I couldn't see much at all. The rear of the house is burned up worse than the front. There's nothing left back there but sky. If she's in there, I can't tell. I need to get the county fire guys out here."

"Oh, Janet's room is upstairs," Sunshine chimed in. We turned slowly, staring at what was left of the second story. Wherever she might have been when the fire started, clearly Janet was no longer upstairs.

The night around us had suddenly grown eerie. The rain was soaking through our many layers of clothes, and we all wished we were somewhere else. At the same time, some of us did not really want to go home alone.

CHAPTER TWO

"We've gotta get the county out here. Probably the sheriff will wanna do some investigatin' too. This is too much for us to handle," Raymond admitted quietly. "Freda, can I use your phone? Dick, Ernie, I want you to go round back. Make sure there's nothin' burning in the brush or under the trees. The last thing we need is for this fire to blow up the canyon. Look around out there for signs of Will and Janet too. Maybe they went out the back door when this thing blew up. Don't go near the house. Just see what you can find." Dick and Ernie took shovels off the truck. They stumbled into the darkness of the hillside behind the house, headlamps bobbing around the trees and underbrush.

"Oh, yes, of course, of course. Everyone, come in, come inside. Come out of the rain," Freda said.

I got the dogs out of the car, let them sniff around, then settled them on the porch furniture where I knew they'd end up anyway, tying them loosely. Most neighbors had already drifted off into the night. Sunshine and Betsy remained together on the dimly lit porch, whispering conspiratorially, waiting for a ride home. Freda herded Raymond, Helen, Nina, and Lauren in the door. After peeling off my wet jacket and draping it on the railing, I followed the others inside.

Freda's smallish bungalow is decorated with furniture, carpets, art, and collectibles brought with her from "the old country," including a glass-fronted cabinet displaying many dozens of tiny Hummel figurines. This was only the second time I had ever been inside. Stepping through the door, I felt like I'd entered a museum. The sweet fragrance of warming strudel wafted into the living room. By the time I came in, Freda had already shown Raymond to the phone mounted in a cubby adjacent to the kitchen door and hustled the others into the kitchen. "I'll put the coffeepot on, then let's get you that strudel," she announced from the kitchen.

Curiosity stopped me at the glass cabinet. What looked like old military decorations were laid carefully on the top shelf at the feet of some of the porcelain figurines. Again I looked around the living room. Ornate polished silver frames held photographs of chubby babies in too-tight old-fashioned woolen jackets buttoned up to their chins. Several hand-painted tea cups with saucers were displayed in another case. The porcelain lamp bases were intricately decorated with images of tiny flowers twining against white backgrounds.

In the hall, an elaborate coat of arms lighted by a small spotlight caught my attention. I knew I was snooping, but couldn't resist a closer look. Next to the fierce red lion coat of arms were several black and white photographs framed by dark wood. In the first, a uniformed officer smiled genially from under thick muttonchops complemented by a neatly trimmed beard. He wore a fez-style hat with a thin bill. His double-breasted jacket boasted brass buttons, a variety of decorations, and several medals. A dark cape was draped around his shoulders and a large cross pattee pinned to the high collar under his chin. A small brass plate at the bottom of the frame simply said "The Duke." Freda is in her late sixties, so this picture was too old to be a husband. Maybe a father or grandfather? I was all set to take a good long gander at the other photographs hung beside that one when the kitchen door swung outward. Freda, holding aloft a very large knife, gave me a stern and suspicious look. All she said was "Are you coming?"

With three others already crowded into the kitchen helping Freda make coffee and serve strudel, I wedged myself into a chair at the small round table. Nina dragged a fifth chair in from the other room. Helen finished setting up the coffeepot, and Freda turned to us, still waving her knife. In her exotic red-patterned caftan with dramatically painted lips, I wondered, not for the first time, if the rumors about her having some kind of theatrical background were true.

"Who is having strudel?" she sang, adding, "It's my mother's best *apfelstrudel* recipe."

"I'm going to lose ten pounds or die trying," Nina rolled her eyes. "Only a very tiny piece for me."

"What?" cried Freda "You're a slip of a thing already! You'll have the biggest slice. And vanilla ice cream too!" She proceeded to serve each of us generous slices of strudel with dollops of ice cream on top while Helen ferried over delicate china cups filled with steaming coffee.

Not trying to disguise our curiosity, we strained to hear Raymond's end of the phone conversation through the swinging kitchen door. He got easier to hear as his frustration became more apparent. There seemed to be some problem with getting someone from the county offices out to Arroyo Loco to examine the fire scene on a rainy Friday night. Mainly what we heard was increasing annoyance peppered with questions like: "What did you say they're doing? Where are they?" and "Well, when do you think they can get here?" Then he started mumbling intensely. None of us could make out anything, even Freda, who by then had stepped close, leaning her head and listening intently. She glanced at us, pursed her lips, and shook her head "no" quickly, then bent again to listen.

That was about the time we heard the phone slammed down, and Raymond tried to enter the kitchen, pushing the door right into Freda's forehead. Bam! That was embarrassing. Raymond looked at her hard for a second, clearly not thinking an apology was in order, at least not from his end.

"Might not be able to get anybody out here for quite awhile tonight," he grumbled, still staring at Freda. He turned to the rest of us. "Fire marshal only has one investigator left after the budget cuts. Her and the sheriff are off on a sensitivity-training meditation retreat up at Esalen until Monday morning. Some guy is comin' out tonight to secure the area, but he won't get here for a while. Guess I'll be baby-sitting the scene," he finished, his lips pressed in a tense line.

My border collies rarely bark at anything, but suddenly they set up a frantic noise out on the front porch. I launched myself from behind the kitchen table to the porch. Nobody messes with my guys. When I got there, Dick and Ernie were approaching out of the darkness. In their dirty yellow jackets and funny-looking fire hats, it was no wonder Shiner and Scout were startled into a barking alarm, the fur raised on their necks. Raymond, who had followed me, called out, "Everything okay out there?"

"Oh, yeah," Dick huffed, regaining his breath. "There's nothing burning in the yard. Damn, the back of that house is totally gone."

Ernie brought up the rear. "That's not all either. Look what we found!" He held up a bright red plastic gasoline can triumphantly. "Found it in the weeds out near that big oak."

"Geez!" Raymond's voice went up about two octaves. "What're you doing handlin' that? That's evidence!"

Ernie dropped his arm, looking in surprise at the offending hand holding the fire can. "Oops," was all he could say.

"Put that damn thing down!" Raymond trotted down the steps and pointed at the ground in front of Ernie. "You guys go on home," he said, including Sunshine and Betsy in his wave. "I gotta stay here to keep an eye on this mess until somebody from the county gets here." As they all moved away, I returned slowly inside, my head swirling. An empty gas can found behind the house must surely mean someone had torched the place. When it comes to means, motive, and opportunity, nearly every person living in Arroyo Loco had all three. So who would take it so far as to burn down the Rosenblums'?

I stepped through Freda's softly lighted living room and into the kitchen, still wondering. The women crowded around the table looked up expectantly when I pushed through. I returned their stares. Silently, Lauren slid into the chair behind the table, Nina slid over one, and I sank into Nina's still-warm place. With Helen taking up most of the rest of the table, Freda eased herself into the chair beside mine. I watched the faces of each of the four other women as I spoke.

"Dick and Ernie found an empty gas can in the weeds behind Will's house. Raymond will have it inspected for fingerprints tomorrow." I didn't say anything about the part where Ernie probably irretrievably smudged any fingerprints that might have been on the can. I watched for responses, every face suddenly the face of a potential arsonist.

It might seem a bit harsh that I should be sitting around a kitchen table sharing a pot of coffee and a nice apple strudel with four women, any one of whom I suspected might be an arsonist. On the other hand, each of us had been so mad at Will about something, probably more than once, that we might have considered burning down his house. Before passing judgment, one has to know the whole story of how we came to be sitting there in Freda's kitchen that night.

"Ah, then it was arson?" Lauren peered at me, her eyes wide and distorted through her thick plastic lenses. Lauren may be a small woman, but she has a powerful brain. Studious and thoughtful, she edits technical journals at home in her office upstairs with windows surveying the canyon of Arroyo Loco. Her housemate, Valerie, rarely comes out of the house. She seems to require Lauren's constant attention.

There was silence around the table. "Maybe," I started. "Then again, maybe that can has been out there for weeks."

"Yes," Nina cut me a sideways look. "Or maybe Will was trying to burn the weeds again. Maybe he set his own house on fire."

"Actually, that sounds exactly like something Will would do," Helen said. Employed for years as a librarian at the nearby state prison, Helen maintains a consistently cynical outlook on human nature. This time there was a murmuring of agreement from around the table.

"Yeah," I nodded. "But if that's what happened, then where is he now? Or, for that matter, where is Janet? I mean, what if they're in there now?"

We sat chewing our strudel over that for a moment. Too horrible to contemplate. Anyway, don't people just come running out screaming when their house catches on fire? Don't we all imagine ourselves running out screaming, carrying the cat and our photograph albums?

Lauren lifted her cup to her lips, returned it the saucer, then looked around. "If it was arson, and if Will and Janet aren't here, then who set their house on fire?" Suspicious glances shot around the table. Okay, so the possible whereabouts of the homeowners being too grim to think about, let's consider the question of who started the fire. Interesting that I wasn't the only one wondering if I was sitting there with someone upset enough to set a neighbor's house ablaze.

A sneer crossed Helen's face as, placing her hand on her forehead, she said, "Okay, I'm channeling here. Sunshine is right! Our collective wishes traveled through time and space to magically manifest themselves in a fire on Will's rear porch."

"More like our collective wishes manifested in a rusty gas can," Lauren expressed her skepticism.

Eyes snapped around to Lauren. "Now, how do you know it's a rusty gas can?" Nina asked in a shrill voice. There were murmurings of agreement. Next, she flashed accusing eyes to Helen. "While we're at it, how do you know the fire started on the rear porch?" Then she turned to me with a puzzled look. "Come to think of it, what were you doing way down in front of my house when the alarm went off?"

"Remember, I was walking the dogs?" I replied quickly. I shot her a scowl. What was she thinking?

Skinny Nina took another bite of her strudel, then slid the rest in front of me. Seriously, just because I'm beginning to look like a plump strudel, why does everyone assume I want seconds? I picked up my fork and dug in.

Nina slid a glance sideways to me again. "No, I mean if you were down in front of my house when the alarm went off, wouldn't you have been more-or-less walking right past when the fire was starting? Didn't you see anything?"

This conversation was getting awkward fast, as suspicious glances flashed among us again. "Hang on a second. Let's don't go off on each other," I protested. "Everybody in this town had some kind of issue with Will. Anyone could have splashed around some gasoline and started that fire. Anyway, it wasn't a rusty gas can. It was a new plastic can. And no, I didn't see anything." I finished, somewhat lamely.

"Stel's right," Helen said, munching a bite. "Anybody could have started that fire. So who would have a strong enough motive?"

"Ah," Lauren started quietly. "Valerie and I did have that huge fight with Will a couple of months ago when we caught him spraying ant poison around our front porch." She paused. "Valerie almost burst a blood vessel, she was so mad. He said he started spraying on his front porch, then he followed the line of ants all the way to our front porch."

"That's a lot of ants," Freda murmured. The rest of us nodded grimly into our coffee cups. Rising, Freda bustled around pouring more coffee as we traded the sugar bowl, tiny milk pitcher, and cut-rate nondairy creamer canister to each other. Lauren passed her plate to me for more strudel. I tried to move Freda's chair over so I could get out to get Lauren's strudel. One leg locked up behind a leg on Helen's chair. We really were jammed in here. I waited to hand Lauren's plate to Freda.

"Two shakes," I assured Lauren.

"What?" She was confused.

"You know, two shakes of a lamb's tail?" Still no comprehension. "It's an old idiom. It means I'll be really quick about it. Have you ever seen a lamb shake it's tail?"

"It's quick?"

"Very. Flick, flick. In the blink of an eye." Being border collies, Shiner and Scout spend their weekdays on a working sheep ranch. In the spring, tiny lambs scamper across the fields after their mothers, shaking their tails and filling the air with their bleating calls.

Four sets of eyes stared at me. Nevermind. Freda handed Lauren's plate back, heaping with another serving of strudel and ice cream, then sat down again.

"Ah, then, anyway," Lauren went on, "we don't really have a motive to burn his place down because Valerie has decided we're moving. We've already started packing." Lauren was referring to her long-time companion, Valerie, who was so reclusive most of us had spoken to her only rarely.

"Oh, no! You're moving?" I said in alarm. Although she was rarely available to sit for a chat, Lauren was one of my favorite neighbors.

"Valerie is so angry at Will. She can't get past it. There was the ant poison. Also, a few weeks ago we had finally finished painting the porch furniture. We'd left it out front to dry. Will was fussing with the sprinklers and sprayed water all over everything. The paint job was ruined. Everything will have to be sanded and repainted. Anyway, Valerie has convinced herself life would be better if we lived somewhere else, so we have to pick up and move. This isn't the first time."

It did seem like Lauren and Valerie moved around a lot. They had lived in Arroyo Loco less than a year, in Berkeley for a couple of years before that, then somewhere near Santa Cruz for a year before that.

"It must be very disruptive for your business to keep moving," I said. Lauren nodded, staring glumly out the window. I cut Nina a sideways glance, curious if I was the only one wondering if Valerie might still be mad enough at Will to torch his house.

Helen began to enumerate on her fingers. "Okay, well, Dick and Betsy have motive because Will set their fence on fire and could have burned down their house. Lauren and Valerie have motive because he sprayed poison around their house and his behavior is driving them out of Arroyo Loco. Or at least Lauren has motive because if Will is gone, she won't have her life disrupted again. So, what about the rest of you? Come on Stel, you're the psychologist. You must have some ideas about motive."

"There's Freda's dead magnolia," I recalled.

"Oh, yes, my dear, dead magnolia tree," Freda sighed deeply. We considered that for a minute. It was really hard to imagine anyone intentionally setting fire to a neighbor's house to retaliate for murdering a tree.

"Maybe Freda put a paper bag of flaming dog poop on the rear porch and it got out of control?" I suggested. Freda startled, turned to stare at me, her eyes wide. Helen laughed out loud, and feminine little Nina snorted so hard, if she'd been drinking milk it would have spurted out her nose.

Lauren looked at us harder. "Really? Flaming dog poop?" She was clearly baffled.

I reached across the table to pat her hand, assuring her, "I'm kidding. I'm sure Freda didn't do that." I could tell Lauren still didn't get it.

Helen came up with another unwelcome suggestion. "Stel, we all know how pissed off you got when Will went in your gate to what, fix the sprinklers back there? You said he was peering in your windows? What about that other time when he left the gate open? Remember, your dogs came running down the canyon looking for you?"

"Yes," Nina laughed. "Then Amanita got her car out and tried to hit them? That's when she drove into the ditch." I did not join in with the general chuckling, although I could see where, if the dogs had not been mine, the story might have been somewhat more entertaining.

Sneering again, Helen chimed in, "Yes, then she tried to get the community to officially scold anyone who let their dogs run loose." Shaking her head, she added, "What a witch." That seemed to sober everyone up. "Still, Stel, I think you have a better motive." She gave me the ole stink eye.

"Well, what about you with your cats?" I snapped back. Last year Helen asked the HOA for permission to build a large wire enclosure onto the front of her house so her many cats could get some fresh air in safety. Will gave an impassioned speech at a community meeting about preserving our precious property values, which, since the California real estate bubble had already burst, left most of us rolling our eyes and asking, "What property values?" Unfortunately for Helen, many pair of rolling eyes were not enough to overcome the objections to her cat box and the project was voted down. Subsequently, several of us were cited for rolling our eyes. It is against community rules to intentionally roll one's eyes to express disapproval during any meeting. I am not kidding here; that rule is written into the community bylaws. This has become quite a handicap for those of us for whom raising our eyebrows to express disbelief and rolling our eyes to express—I don't know, whatever rolling one's eyes expresses—form a significant part of our usual set of communication skills. Mumbling under one's breath along with audible expressions such as "Oh, pluuu-eeze!" are also banned during meetings.

"Well, I have motive too," Helen agreed. "Except it would be more my style to strangle the old coot with my bare hands."

Nina nodded solemnly while we contemplated that visual. "Yes. You bring up a good point, Helen," she said. "Will has made plenty of enemies here in Arroyo Loco, although burning down his house does seem a bit over the top for anyone. But it's Janet's house too. Who would want to burn down Janet's house, or hurt her?"

"Oh, you're right," Freda agreed. "We don't any of us know her well, but she seems so sweet."

"Do you know her, Freda?" I asked.

"I think she has that old-timer's disease. You can't talk to her so much," Freda sighed. "Will keeps her locked up most of the time. He says she wanders if he lets her out. He used to bring her to Saturday coffee sometimes. She only smiles and nods. She was better when they first moved here. Lately, I don't know, maybe not so good."

Helen's bulk leaned eagerly across the table, "Okay, so Will really did burn the house down to put Janet out of her misery."

Yeah, now we were getting somewhere. Burning down the house for a reason like that does make sense. Not a lot, I'll admit, but some. Also, it was a lot easier to believe Will did it himself than to think about who else might have done such a thing.

"Or to collect the insurance so he could afford to put her in a home or something like that," Lauren added, more reasonably.

"Of course!" I agreed. "That makes sense!"

"Yes. Maybe it was one of those awful murder/suicide things," Nina said in a shocked whisper. I slid her a look, but couldn't tell if she was serious.

Helen glowered at her from across the table. "Okay, well, somebody's been watching too much television," she muttered grimly. Nina pretended not to hear that one.

I thought about all of those suggestions. "So, what it really comes down to is that even with all the enemies Will has made here, the only person in Arroyo Loco who we think might really have done such a terrible thing is Will himself. Is that what we're saying?"

Nina nodded. "Yes. It's the only rational explanation."

I cut her a look again. Was she serious this time? With Nina, it's so hard to tell. "Hmm, maybe," I said. "Seriously though, there are not many circumstances where burning down a house could be considered a rational act. Will burning his own house down for the insurance money might make for a believable television movie, but that doesn't make it rational. Given what I've learned about Will's behavior, I would have to say schizotypal personality disorder, probably of the negativistic type, which makes setting fire to the house more a manifestation of mental illness than a rational act." There was silence around the table. I was getting that psychologist-has-gone-too-far-with-the-professional-lingo look.

"Well, somebody burned down the house, and believe it or not, I think Will did it himself," Helen said. "If he didn't do it, who did?" She looked hard across the table at Nina. "We haven't talked about you, Nina. What would be your motive? What has Will done that got you pissed off enough to burn down his house?"

Nina raised her eyebrows and opened her eyes wide as we all turned to stare at her. "Me?" she squeaked. "Me? I've never had any problem with Will!"

The rest of us continued to look at her in silence. She was the very picture of innocence. On the other hand, really, it was true. In public, Nina was as sweet as pie. She never had words with anyone. Although she could be as snarky as any of us in private, now that I thought about it, she was never in the middle of any of the big fights around here. I wondered how she managed to pull that off. All by itself, that was a little suspicious. She picked up her cup and took a sip, her pinky slightly extended.

"Why does it have to be someone in town?" asked Lauren. "Why can't it be a stranger?"

Freda raised one doubtful eyebrow, "Oh, you mean a complete stranger, like a hitch-hiker off the highway?"

"Why not? I'd rather it'd be somebody like that than one of us!" Lauren was defensive.

"Yes, but think about it Lauren," reasoned Nina. "Some stranger would have to walk up the canyon past ten or twelve other houses, carrying a full gas can ..."

"Yeah, then what?" Helen jumped in. "He picks that place at random and torches it?" Then she had a second thought. "Could someone have come across the ridge from behind?"

"Maybe, but you still have the problem of motive," I pointed out. "I mean, unless it was a completely random act."

The cuckoo in Freda's dining room began to chime and chime and chime. "Good grief! What time is it?" Lauren's mouth dropped open. "Ah! Valerie's going to kill me!"

"Eleven!" we all counted. Since Lauren was in the chair behind the small wooden table, we all had to get up to let her out. Everyone gathered up dishware while I quickly washed and stacked them in the drainer. Freda rummaged around in a drawer looking for a flashlight for Helen, who had the most treacherous walk home in the dark. She found one, then ushered us out. We shrugged into coats, gathered up umbrellas, and plopped on hats. The rain had long since stopped falling, leaving the air steamy. Or maybe that was smoke. Elf-like, Lauren tripped down the steps off into the night toward her house next door. Clomping more troll-like down the steps, Helen trudged off along the driveway, her raincoat flapping. Long after the rest of her disappeared into the darkness, the wavering flashlight danced under her bleached bob, marking her way. As I watched Helen go, I thought about how whatever evil the fire may have wrought that night, it had also brought some of us closer together in friendship.

Nina and I collected our own things including my two dogs. Their black and white fur stark in the darkness, the dogs yawned, stretched, and lifted their noses to the night air. It was heavy with the smell of wood smoke, burned plastic, and other less identifiable scents.

"Hmm. I guess that's it then, isn't it?" I said. "Will set fire to his own house, burning it to the ground." We stared bleakly at the dark skeleton of remains. The fire engine was still parked there. We could make out Raymond's head with the fire hat pulled low over his eyes, slouched in the driver's seat.

Nina put her hand to her mouth, yawning daintily. "Yes, Will's only lucky he didn't burn the whole canyon down. Imagine what a disaster it could have been!" She flashed a guilty smile, "I mean, more of a disaster."

"That's true," I agreed. "Anyone who would set any kind of a fire in this canyon would have to be a few cards short of a full deck, or be truly evil." I stood there for a few moments looking up the oak-studded canyon. My house was still out of sight around the bend in the road. I shuddered again, thinking what might have happened if that fire had gotten out of control.

I was stowing the dogs into Nina's car when she said, "Hey, let's go see what's up with Raymond." She headed that direction. I told the dogs to wait, closed the car door, then followed her carefully across the darkened road, gravel crunching under my feet.

The cab light in the fire engine blinked on as we approached, and the door squealed open. Raymond swiveled slowly, his unlaced boots coming to rest on the step about level with our knees. With one grimy hand, he pushed his hat back. "Ladies," he said.

"Hi, Raymond. How are you holding up?" Nina smiled, batting her eyelashes, a gesture doubtlessly wasted in the darkness.

"Oh." He sighed deeply. "Waitin' on somebody from the county." He rested his elbow on the steering wheel and his dark eyes shifted in the direction of the house.

"You have to wait here all night? The fire's out now, right?" I inquired, still thinking about my close call.

"Oh, yeah." He sighed again. "Looks like the fire's out all right. We still need somebody official out here, you know. Looks like arson, so we need somebody from the county out to secure the scene. Yellow tape and all that jazz. Guy I talked to said he'd need to stop at maintenance, pick up some lights, so that's probably why he's late gettin' here."

We were all trying not to breathe too deeply, being that close to the house. What was that strange smell? Nina glanced at the house, then at Raymond. "We talked about it and decided if it was arson, Will must have started the fire himself. You know, like for the insurance money or something like that?"

Raymond pushed his hat farther back and scratched his close-cropped hair, leaving a streak of wetness across his forehead. He gave us a long look. "Well, now, I don't see how that can be so."

Nina and I stood in silence, letting the question hang in the night air. Sounded like Raymond knew more than he was saying. After a few seconds he went on.

"I don't want this gettin' around tonight. It'll scare people. We won't know anything more until the fire marshal and the county coroner can investigate anyways."

He had me at the word coroner. Nobody calls a coroner for an arson fire unless there's a dead body. Except for a slight intake of breath from Nina, we let the silence among us continue. Then I thought, oh yeah, now that you mention it, maybe that is what that smell is about. I decided not to say anything. I was already a little queasy.

Raymond turned his eyes away from us again, staring through the dusty windshield. "Will is in there, in the back bedroom."

At the same time both Nina and I raised our hands to our mouths, moving closer together. Wish I hadn't eaten so much strudel. I turned so the burned house wasn't in my direct line of sight. Nina looked like she was also wishing she'd wake up from what felt like a very bad dream.

Raymond glanced down at us apologetically. "I'm sorry. I shouldn't have said anything. Didn't mean to upset you ladies."

"Yes, of course," Nina whispered. Then, "Really?" She paused again. "Are you sure it's Will?"

Raymond slid down off the truck seat and hit the ground. He lifted the heavy hat off, placing it on the cracked vinyl seat. "Oh, yeah, it's a long, tall, skinny guy lying on what's left of a steel bed frame there in the back bedroom. Gruesome if you want the truth." He swiped his hand across his forehead, then waved it toward the ashes. "Looks like, smells like, there was gasoline poured all around that side of the house. Place more or less went off like a bomb, startin' in the back there."

"He's lying there on the bed?" Nina was incredulous. "He didn't try to get out?"

"Nope. Just lyin' there," Raymond confirmed.

It was about then that I stumbled over to the ditch at the edge of the asphalt and lost all those strudel calories I had unwisely consumed. Dead people might be standard fare every evening in living rooms across America, but it's different in real life, especially when it's an acquaintance.

Worse if it's an acquaintance one dislikes, or wishes was dead.

Raymond walked Nina toward her car where I joined them. He put a hand on each of our shoulders. "Listen, it's late. You ladies should get on home. We'll get this sorted out in the morning."

I wasn't really in the mood to argue. "Yes, but what about you?" Nina asked. "Are you okay out here? Do you want some company? Can I get you a cup of coffee or something?"

"No, no. I don't need anything, thanks for the offer. We'll get the county on out here sometime tonight. They'll look around. At least get that body out of here." He looked over his shoulder. "Probably be back in the morning. See if they can figure out what happened. It's out of our hands now."

I went around the car and got in, still feeling shaky. After a few minutes Nina slid into the driver's seat and buckled her seat belt. The question of motive was still eating at me, more so now that the crime appeared to be deadly serious. When we pulled into my driveway I turned toward her. "So, Nina, you know when there was that proposal to install a gate across the entrance to Arroyo Loco right near your house? You got upset because it would be opening and closing at all hours? Wasn't that Will's idea? He wanted to keep Janet from wandering onto the highway or something? Weren't you really angry about that?"

Nina's eyes narrowed, but she didn't miss a beat. "Oh no, that was Brycie. We'd had all those thefts of bikes and patio stuff. Bryce wanted to turn us into a gated community. Remember, he got all weepy at that one meeting about he was only trying to protect his dear parents?" At 29, Bryce still lives with his parents, Ernie and Alice, in their converted garage.

I nodded slowly. "So, it wasn't Will?"

"No, that was Bryce. Maybe Will too. They like to stick together. You are right about me being angry. I was mad as a wet hen. Can you imagine? That gate would have been right outside my bedroom window, opening and closing every time anyone drove in or out of the canyon! Anyway the gate never happened, so that's not much of a motive."

"No, I guess not," I agreed.

The dogs and I got out and went straight through the screened porch and off to bed. With the help of a small pharmaceutical intervention, I eventually fell into a dreamless sleep.

CHAPTER THREE

As it turned out, Nina did not go directly home. She told me the next morning that she stopped again in front of the burned house. She sat there in her car watching. First the white sedan with the county fire marshal's seal on the door arrived, then the dark van from the coroner's office. Several people suited up in what looked like hazmat gear clambered around what was left of the Rosenblums' house, powerful flashlight beams sweeping the wreckage. Many photographs were taken, the flash from the camera making lightning bolts against the cloudy night sky. After another hour or so, a gurney was wheeled around to the rear porch. Sometime later the hazmat suits returned, struggling across the rough ground with a long black bag strapped on top of the aluminum gurney, loaded it into the van and drove away. Nina's description of the scene was dramatic but incomplete. I learned later that she left a significant detail or two out of her account.

Saturday morning dawned brilliant and clear, that kind of stunning deep blue, with towering white pillows of cumulus clouds floating slowly past my window. I am not the sort of person who bounds out of bed at sunrise, happy to be alive. By the time I reached full consciousness, I was remembering the fire and the body found afterwards. The idea of a murder by arson was certainly horrifying. Heaven knows, I wouldn't wish that on anyone. At the same time, if someone here had to die and it was up to me to choose who, Will would definitely be on my list. By all accounts including his own, he spent most of his life making other people miserable. He told someone once that his older brother tormented him mercilessly when he was a child. That was his excuse for making life hard for everyone around him. I'm sorry he was apparently mistreated, if that's genuinely the way it happened. On the other hand, maybe Will was an annoying obnoxious kid from the start, and his brother only tormented him out of self-defense. It could have happened either way.

On the brighter side, Arroyo Loco was going to be a different, and I sincerely hoped, a more pleasant place to live with Will gone. There was still the mystery of how it had happened, but in the cheery light of a new morning, that all seemed like an interesting puzzle to work out and no longer a thing ominous or scary.

The gravel in my driveway crunched, the screen door squealed, and someone banged on my kitchen door. I did leap out of bed then, shrugged into my bathrobe and ran fingers through my hair as I headed for the kitchen. Glancing out the dining area window on my way, I saw a county sheriff's SUV parked across my driveway, leaning slightly toward the ditch. Uh-oh.

I didn't know the uniformed and heavily muscled man standing in my screened porch, so when he slurred his name and inquired if he could, "Please ask you some questions ma'am?" I gestured toward the wicker chairs out on the porch. His khaki shirt was starched and carefully pressed, a brass badge shiny in the morning sun. I caught a whiff of manly-scented soap whenever he moved. Persuading my wiggling and reluctant-to-leave dogs through their dog door into the backyard, I slid the panel in place to keep them there. Scout, always the brains in this outfit, ran out to the corner post, snaked through the hole he'd worked in the fence, trotted to the officer's SUV and lifted his leg on a tire. Oh, man. Still facing me, Deputy Mumble missed the action. I perched on the edge of a flowered cushion while he pulled a small notebook with a stubby pencil from his shirt pocket and sat down opposite me.

"Okay, ma'am," he began, "I understand you were present when the fire started at the Rosenblum home last night. Can you tell me what you were doing there?" He looked down at his notebook, prepared to inscribe my answer.

Now see, this is what I mean about the rumor mill at Arroyo Loco. Somehow, between last night and this morning, we had gone from me innocently walking my dogs past the house, to me being present at the scene of a murder and arson. Not only that, but now I needed an explanation for my highly suspect presence there. I wondered which one of my strudel-snacking companions had hatched this version of my activities.

I stared hard at him, willing his dark eyes to meet mine, but he was fixed on his little notebook. "No," I replied in an unintentionally snarky tone. Probably not my most diplomatic move. I decided to try another tack. "I mean, I wasn't there when the fire started."

He said, "Right," looking down again at his notebook. I noticed he wasn't writing anything.

"No, really," I assured him. "I didn't know anything about the fire until the alarm went off. I was down by the roadhouse when that happened. Maybe about a quarter after nine?"

Okay, that sounded incriminating. I tried again. "Look, I left here about eight thirty and walked the dogs slowly down canyon to that park across from the fire engine garage. We hung around there for fifteen or twenty minutes, then we continued on down to the roadhouse. I was starting up canyon when the alarm went off. I didn't see anything out of the ordinary on my way past Will's house." That was almost the whole truth.

"I see." The deputy was apparently not much of a Chatty Cathy. At least now he was scribbling frantically. "Okay. What were you doing hanging around the park?"

Oh geez, now he's got me hanging around the park suspiciously. I sighed silently, trying not to roll my eyes. "Letting my dogs sniff around." That sounded a little cryptic. I pulled the neck of my bathrobe tighter and tried again. "You know, letting the dogs take care of business."

"Letting your dogs sniff around," he repeated slowly as he carefully noted this fact. "Taking care of business."

"I clean up after them," I pointed out. He was starting to make me nervous. It didn't help that the rules of the HOA prohibited dogs in the empty lot beside the Carpers' house. That lot had originally been designated as a park and playground for Arroyo Loco, but for years Betsy had objected to every proposal to install play equipment for even the smallest children, or any other use for the space. She'd had her husband, Dick, plant a poor quality grass seed on part of the area, and he mowed it regularly. In a moment of magnanimity, the Carpers purchased a picnic table with benches, but anyone who tried to use the park for any purpose other than sitting quietly was promptly chased off for fear they would disturb Betsy by making noise of some sort. Expressly forbidden by the rules of the HOA was the installation, even temporarily, of items such as sheets over the table to make a "fort" for the children, or almost needless to say, the presence of dogs.

"I always clean up after them. You'd never know they had ever been there," I assured the deputy.

Still looking at his notebook, he scratched his forehead. He decided not to jot that part down, slapped the notebook closed and slipped it in his shirt pocket. With the hint of an apology in his voice, and without making eye contact, he said, "Listen, both senior detectives are out of town this weekend. I'm filling in here. The damage is already done, whatever evidence was left is already collected. I'm no fire inspector, so we'll let this go until next week. Sheriff's detective will probably come around on Monday if he has any more questions. In the meantime, don't leave town without letting us know." He handed me a small white card and his eyes finally met mine for the briefest of seconds. Wow, exactly like on television! What was I here, a suspect?

He stood, turned to go, then stopped, cutting me a look. "Oh, one more question." Very Columbo-like. "Any idea as to the whereabouts of Mrs. Rosenblum? That would be Wilhelm's wife, Janet."

I shook my head "No, no idea. I didn't know them. Well, hardly at all."

He nodded once, then added, "Okay, well, call the office if you think of anything else." As he turned the sunlight hit his name tag, and I could finally read his name: Antonio Muñoz. The screen door squealed again as he let himself out.

Quickly running water into a plastic bucket, I followed him down the steps. As he got in and buckled up, I sloshed water on his tire, trying to erase Scout's calling card. It took the deputy about three tries to get that big SUV turned around heading down canyon. Then he gunned it, roaring off in a very masculine way. I put down the bucket and waved goodbye in what I hoped looked like a very innocent- and honest-citizen way. After that, I went to the hole Scout had used to make his escape and tried to pull the wire around to make a temporary patch.

Wandering onto to the porch, I curled up again in the wicker chair, watching the dogs romp with each other. Let me be very clear right from the outset here. I am no Hercule Poirot. I'm not even an Inspector Clouseau. But it was scary how suspicion in the case of the fire in Arroyo Loco, and the gruesome death of at least one of its residents seemed to be falling in my direction. If another villain could not be apprehended or at least identified quickly, I was going to find myself in quite a pickle. Up a canyon without an alibi, one might say.

After all, it was true that I had been walking right past the house at almost the exact time the fire must have started. Equally true, although I'd not mentioned this to anyone else yet, when we reached Will's driveway last night, my dogs took off toward the rear of the house as though in pursuit of a rabbit or something running. They went in silence and returned about two minutes later, still in silence. I didn't think too much about it at the time, and kept walking.

So, as far as I knew, I was the only suspicious character lurking around Will's house last night. If I couldn't figure out who committed this crime and get myself off the hook,

I might end up in serious trouble. Although unqualified to conduct such an inquiry, I certainly had motivation, and this morning that would have to be enough.

To get started, I would need to bring myself up to speed on the rumors circulating in Arroyo Loco that morning. There was no better way to do that than to overcome my natural reluctance and attend the Saturday morning coffee klatch and weekly gossip gathering at the roadhouse. I decided to take the dogs to the beach, stopping off at the roadhouse on the way.

I called Nina first to make sure at least one friendly face would be there. We chatted for a while, then I got dressed. Land's End chino shorts and a polo shirt for the preppy look. My specially engineered running shoes for the serious runner part. I'm not a serious or even not-so-serious runner. I found the shoes on sale at the Northface outlet store in Berkeley last spring. Nevertheless, sometimes I wish I was a runner, and you never know when I might take it up, so I like to at least look the part. I donned my Giants baseball cap in lieu of doing anything with my hair, a futile effort anyway, as we were going to the beach. That should do it. Oh, and my Cal State San Benito zip-up sweatshirt for the intellectual part. Also in case the beach was cooler or windy.

I backed my beat-up green Subaru wagon out of the driveway, being careful not to crush the bucket I'd left there. As we coasted slowly down the narrow lane, I tried to avoid looking in the direction of the still slightly steaming pile of wreckage. The bright yellow crime scene tape was hard to ignore. It was staked to enclose all the yard area in front of the house, but for some reason did not extend out around the freestanding garage. Looking ahead, a haze of white smoke lay low over the houses below. The air held a steely, wet ash fragrance.

Not surprisingly, the group sitting on the roadhouse porch was larger than usual. Seven or eight of the regulars had gathered, plus several others. Ever notice how certain people can't stand to miss a party? Some of the tables and rickety chairs had been pulled out onto the wide porch, and I radared in on a big pink bakery box on a table outside the door. As I cruised slowly past on my way to the parking area I spotted a couple of friendly faces including Nina, Helen, and further down, Freda. Scattered among these, there were also some sour, unfriendly faces. Amanita's distinctive mushroom-shaped head with the bowl-like haircut caught my eye. She stood at the end of the tables, pontificating about something. Who knew what? In her own mind she was an expert on everything, so it was hard to say what she might be lecturing about this morning. An early morning encounter with Amanita wasn't high on my wish list.

On the other hand, there was the bakery box. Okay, I'll stop. I left the car in the deep shade of an oak with the windows rolled down, the dogs asleep inside. Walking back, I climbed the worn steps to the porch, my social anxiety kicking into high gear. I almost never attend the Saturday coffee klatch.

The conversation quieted, and peals of laughter faded as I reached the group. Silence. I nodded to my right toward heavy-lidded Marla, a highly observant and calculating woman in her 40s. Calculating both literally and figuratively; she works as a tax attorney at a high-end firm in Atascadero. Marla plays everything close to the vest. On the rare occasions when she does speak, she has a rapier-like wit and a vicious tongue. She'll always get my vote for the Most Likely to Back-stab a Neighbor for Her Own Gain title. Of course, here in Arroyo Loco competition for that distinction is stiff, with plenty of deserving contenders. I thought it wise to let Marla know I saw her sitting there. She sneered in return, and looked away. From down the table farther right, Bryce gave me a pious tightlipped smile.

"Good news, Estela!" Nina called from the other end of the tables. "Janet's been located, safe and sound!" She flapped a dismissive hand in the air, a smile of relief lighting her face, and happy murmurs of agreement from those around her.

"Oh, that's great! I've been so worried!" I chimed in with the mood. "Where did she turn out to be?" I patted Shiner's head as he sidled up to me on the porch. Wait a second, what was he doing there? Darn dog. I tried to pretend he wasn't there. Not surprisingly, it's against the rules to bring a dog to the roadhouse. Lucky for me, Shiner was by himself. Scout, being the older dog, was probably still stretched out enjoying a solitary nap.

Next to me, Betsy glanced up, "Alice took her to the bus station Thursday. She went to Santa Barbara to visit Kenneth." Betsy then shifted her gaze pointedly down to Shiner, who slunk quickly out of sight under a bench.

Ernie's wife, Alice, turned her goofy grin in my direction, her white frizzy hair forming a fluffy puff around her face. "Yes, yes, I took her to the bus station in Atascadero, and stayed until she got on the bus. She's fine." I remembered then that Alice was not among those watching the fire last night. That was a bit odd, since her husband played such a big role in the exciting events of the evening. Still, it was good to know Janet was safely out of town when her home burned down and her husband died.

"Wow, well, that's good," I reiterated. I sidled toward the door into the dining room, dragged out a chair and wedged it in next to Freda. Was it my imagination, or did she ease away from me the tiniest bit? I went back for a chipped cup and weak coffee from the urn on the bar, a paper plate and plastic fork, then cruised past the bakery box, forking up a bear claw on my way.

Conversations resumed once I settled in. As soon as the chatter began again, I leaned in to Freda and tried to whisper, "Who's Kenneth? Has anyone talked to Janet?"

Alice, sitting across from us, overheard and replied, "Kenneth is Janet's brother. She got word he was sick last week. In the hospital. Janet said it was something serious."

I nodded slowly and chewed. Took a sip of coffee. Man, that was foul stuff. Whoever made it had really stinted on the coffee this time. Used tap water, and a paper towel for a filter. Or an old dishrag. I eased the cup away from me so I wouldn't mistakenly take another sip. The bear claw, on the other hand, was quite tasty. I enjoyed another mouthful. "So, has anyone talked to Janet? When is she coming home?"

Again there was silence at our end of the tables. Bryce and Amanita appeared to be engaged in a heated argument down at the other end about whether the fire would have gone up or down canyon if it had gotten out of control last night. Finally, Helen answered me, starting with a question of her own. "Well, do you have any idea how to find Janet?"

Chewing again, I shook my head. "No." Why would anyone think I would have any way of knowing how to contact Janet at her brother's house? I didn't know she had a brother.

"Well, see, that's the thing," Helen continued. "No one knows how to contact her. Nobody here knows if there are other family members somewhere else. No emergency contacts. No records. Nothing is left in the house. No way to identify the body, at least until the lab gets it."

Hmm. That was a puzzle indeed. I considered the problem. What if my house burned to the ground and I got barbecued along with it? Would anyone here know how to find my family or my dental records? This being the twenty-first century, it might seem like a no-brainer to email Janet or send a quick text message, or call her on her cell phone, although if her dementia was as bad as people said, she probably didn't have one. Hardly anyone in Arroyo Loco has a cell phone. We are located in a steep canyon where cell phone signals will not penetrate. People here who do have cell phones have them only for work or for when traveling. We also can't get satellite television. About four years ago we finally did get one company to run a cable line out here. We also have land-based telephones, giving us slow and unreliable dial-up internet access. In any case, if Janet did have a cell phone, no one here had the number.

Contemplating this put me off onto another train of thought. A few months ago, shortly after the Rosenblums arrived, our then-resident techie guy, Dave, Amanita's fiancé, made a proposal to provide us all with wireless access to high-speed internet. He worked with a local company that agreed to run a cable out to Arroyo Loco and install a wireless router on the roof of the roadhouse. The router would beam a signal up canyon, available to every house all the way to Amanita's at the far upper end. The HOA would be billed for the service, and we would all chip in to pay for it, but at a much lower rate than if we each had to pay for internet access individually. It was a great idea, and Dave put together an enthusiastic presentation. He was understandably proud of his proposal.

We held a meeting to vote and went around the circle, each of us congratulating Dave on his hard work and expressing our excitement about this chance to finally join this century. We always sit in a circle at our HOA meetings, allegedly to illustrate our unity and supposed lack of hierarchy. More likely, I think it is so the no rolling-of-eyes and raising-of-eyebrows rules can be enforced. Anyway, we went around the circle and eventually got to Wally. Picture a really skinny Bozo the Clown after he's had way, way too much caffeine. Reddish frizzy hair out to here all around, then completely bald on top, worn-out rumpled baggy clothes, shoes too big, jittery, jumpy, chewing his nails, picking his nose, chewing his nails again. That's Wally. He always smells like old clothes pulled out of the bottom of a dampish box at the thrift store, which his probably were. The gist of his comments at this meeting were that he and his wife, Tina, who was at least twenty years his junior and had never, to my knowledge, ever had an independent idea, were unwilling to pay for the signal. It was pointed out that the cost was probably lower than he was already paying for dial-up, but he was steadfast. After much discussion, including mention of that fact that Wally would have access to the signal whether he paid for it or not, it was finally agreed that households willing to pay would divide the cost amongst themselves, and households unwilling to pay would get the signal for free.

Already this was bad, and then it was Will's turn. This was the first time I had heard his opinion, and since he was a new neighbor, I decided to listen. We all turned around to watch him as he spoke. We had to turn to see him because from his very first meeting, Will refused to sit in the circle. His tall stooping figure lurked in the shadows, pacing as he pulled on the straggly ends of his long gray ponytail. Will's opinion about the wireless plan, which he delivered in a rambling and wheezy monologue, was that we should not accept it. In his view, there was too much danger that the wireless signal being beamed into our homes twenty-four hours a day would disrupt our sleep cycles, cause cell damage and every kind of cancer imaginable, and would give alien invaders free access to corrupt and pollute our brain waves.

I remember sitting in that meeting in disbelief. Was this for real? Was this an insane asylum? Were there really people walking around out there, living amongst us and having an impact on our lives who believed this stuff? I looked at Dave and realized he shared my disbelief. His eyebrows arched and his mouth hung open like he wanted to say something, but nothing was coming out.

Then it got worse. After some shuffling around and a few strictly verboten private conversations, Bryce suggested that, "Since Will feels so strongly, as a community and to honor his presence as a member of that community, we should table the discussion about the wireless system until such time as it can be proven to be completely harmless." There was a virtual epidemic of eye rolling at that point, but we all knew the desire to avoid conflict would override common sense. The inmates had taken over the asylum. The proposal was dropped and hasn't been raised since.

Not too long after that, Dave left our little community, leaving Amanita at the altar as well. I don't think anyone's heard from him, and she's been alone ever since.

As my consciousness slowly returned to last night's fire and the gathering around me, I realized that Amanita might have a better motive to wish Will gone than most other people sitting there this morning. If Will could be made to disappear, maybe Dave would return.

I scraped the last few crumbs from my plate and tuned back into the conversation around the tables. Betsy was announcing that she was going to organize a memorial service for Will. Seemed a little odd to me to be talking about that before anyone had been able to contact Janet, but Betsy was quite excited. Almost, one might say, celebratory. Everyone quieted to hear her plans.

CHAPTER FOUR

"You know," Betsy announced, "it's such a shame Will didn't listen to me. I would have tried to help him find his way here. I would have been willing to show him there were many ways his life in Arroyo Loco could have been a more positive experience. If only he had listened to me. Imagine how I feel now, knowing it's too late for him to hear me and he is gone. It's so frustrating."

She sighed deeply, looking around at each of us in sadness. We stared at her in silence. Yes, indeed, Betsy is definitely the one who should be getting our sympathies here. Will is dead. Janet lost her husband. Betsy is frustrated. Let's get our priorities right. At least that's what I was thinking. A fat, shiny tear rolled down Betsy's freckled cheek.

Have I mentioned that, in our private conversations, we often refer to her as Betsy Wetsy, after the doll? Remember that baby doll, very popular in the '60s? Every girl had one. I have no idea what kinds of dolls kids play with today, but back then toy makers decided we wanted a "realistic" doll. Betsy Wetsy came with a tiny plastic bottle that could be filled up with water and used to "feed" her. There must have been a tube or something inside the doll, because as fast as water dribbled into her mouth, it all dribbled right back out again into your lap from a hole drilled through her anatomically incorrect plastic bottom. Way, way more trouble than she was worth. She required a tiny paper diaper and tiny rubber pants also. And the diaper had to be changed every time she was fed, or she would be found many months later with her tiny moldy diaper stuck to her permanently stained bottom. So, that's why Arroyo Loco's Betsy is called Betsy Wetsy; she's way too high-maintenance. Also, in case it has slipped anyone's attention, everything that happens in Arroyo Loco is, in some way or another, all about Betsy. Or so she sees it.

"I was hoping," she went on, "we could all gather under the trees at the park and I could give a short inspirational talk and read some of my poetry. We could have flowers and maybe Tina could play her flute or some of the children could sing."

The rest of us continued to stare in disbelief. Helen, in particular, turned deliberately and glared at Betsy. "Will hated children," she said in her most cynical and deadpan tone of voice. "He also hated poetry and trees. And he most definitely hated inspirational talks."

Now with two tears sliding toward her chin, Betsy turned a crestfallen face toward Helen. Betsy sniffed, rose gracefully from her chair, and, if a person can be said to flounce in shorts and Birkenstocks, she flounced indignantly across the porch and down the steps, her back turned firmly toward us.

"Anyway," Helen added, watching Betsy go and showing no mercy, "Don't you think we should wait and see if the body turns out to really be Will before we bury it?"

There were small gasps and knit brows all around the tables. "What?" squealed Bryce, placing his fingertips to his tightened lips. "What do you mean, wait and see if it is Will? How could it not be Will?"

"Well, from what I heard that body was one crispy critter. It could have been almost anyone." I cringed. That probably was an apt description of the body, but wow, that Helen could really be insensitive. She went on, "The deputy sheriff said we'd have to wait until next week for it to be positively identified. Without dental records, it'll probably take longer than that. And we know something else." She paused and stared pointedly across the table at Nina, who dropped her gaze and pretended not to notice. "Nina," Helen persisted. "Don't you have something you want to share?" That's when I learned the piece of the story Nina had left out earlier.

Without making eye contact with anyone, Nina glanced around the faces all looking at her. "Ahem." Nina never does anything as coarse as to clear her throat. Instead, she simply says the word, "Ahem." She stared at the table another second or two, then spoke deliberately. "Yes. Well, it seems that last night the young man from the county medical examiner's office who came out to get the body, well, he found a ring in with the, well, with the remains."

Silence. Then, "Will doesn't wear any rings," said Bryce, from the other end of the tables.

"That's what this young man said, or rather he said the ring didn't appear to have been on the hand. It almost fell off when they moved the body," Nina confirmed. People shifted uncomfortably.

"Well, duh," Helen jumped in. "The body was cooked. Of course a ring would fall off if the flesh was all burned off!"

Somebody, maybe it was me, said quietly, "Oh, Helen, for heaven's sake, put a lid on it!" Alice got up and stumbled down the steps after Betsy, looking decidedly green.

"Ahem," Nina went on. "It's a ring from Harvard, class of nineteen something."

"Will didn't go to Harvard," Bryce observed.

"No. No, he didn't," Nina again confirmed. I wondered how she would know that.

"Maybe Janet, or maybe her brother, Kenneth, maybe he went to Harvard," Freda suggested. "Many Jews went to Harvard in those days." Helen shot me a look. Nobody else moved or made a sound for half a minute. We here in Arroyo Loco are a very diverse bunch, but we try to ignore that as best we can. One of the strategies we use, it seems, is to never mention the differences. Like, if we never talk about them, we can pretend they don't exist, or aren't important. Of course the differences—be they ethnic, spiritual, life-style, or whatever—are important but the unwritten rule is never to mention them. Freda had broken that rule. She had the good grace to look embarrassed as she busied herself dusting crumbs in circles in front of her. "I mean the body might be Kenneth," she mumbled.

Abruptly, quiet questions popped up all around, everyone interrupting everyone else. So maybe the body wasn't Will's? Was it the brother who died in the fire last night? How might his body have gotten into Will and Janet's house? If Will isn't dead, where is he? And from somewhere at the other end of the tables, someone asked, "What the heck's up with Freda?"

Finally, Helen spoke loudly over the chatter which gradually quieted. "Well, someone in Arroyo Loco burned down the Rosenblums' house thinking they were getting rid of Will, and instead they killed the wrong person. Will is probably somewhere now laughing his head off at all of us. How's that for a theory?" Helen looked slowly at each person present.

I don't know about anyone else, but my mind was so full of questions, I didn't know what to think. Did Will persuade Janet's brother to come to Arroyo Loco, then kill him? Kenneth was already seriously sick, so maybe he died and Will brought his body here? What would be the point of that? Where was Janet? Was there a chance she had started the fire herself? Could a person with dementia start a fire like that? How do we know Janet has dementia? According to the deputy sheriff, no one from their office would begin to investigate until at least Monday. Janet's life might be in danger now, and no one was looking for her. I wanted to believe that Will was behind the fire, and now also the possible murder, but what if Helen was wrong? What if the villain was someone else, someone here? What might that person do if we started poking around before the sheriff's office began investigating?

I guess I was feeling lucky, and motivated to get information. "We need some answers," I leaned toward Helen. "We at least need to find a way to track down Janet. We need to make sure she's safe wherever she is." Then I realized I wasn't feeling that lucky, so I decided to recruit some companions. "The fire's out. Let's go see if we can find anything else at the house. At the very least we can look around in the garage now that it's light." By this time, everyone was listening. I glanced at faces to see if anyone was looking panicked or villainous. We were all trained so carefully not to roll eyes, raise eyebrows, or otherwise express feelings, all I saw were poker faces. Except for Marla, who was staring at me, her eyes slits of hatred. Then again, that look was typical for Marla. It didn't necessarily mean anything.

Nobody jumped to their feet immediately. I pushed away from the table slightly. There was general movement, the scraping of a few chair legs on the wooden porch, and Helen stood up.

"Stop!" Bryce demanded. "You can't go in there! That's a crime scene!"

Amanita watched in silence. Her life is all about inventing new rules and making other people follow them. If she wanted to join us, and it seemed like she did as she turned and stared up canyon, she couldn't really justify breaking the rules. I knew any minute she was going to start lecturing about why we shouldn't go, so I figured we should skeedadle. Pushing my chair further back, I stood up and looked down at Nina, but she had developed a sudden interest in a hangnail. "Come on, Nina," I whispered urgently.

"I need to finish that color board, Estela. You girls go on ahead. I'll catch up with you later." She waved her hand dismissively, again playing the innocent good girl. Clearly, she wasn't coming.

Freda absentmindedly fanned herself with her hand and glanced around nervously. Freda is generally quite adventurous, so I found her response uncharacteristic. I sent her a puzzled expression, but she also wasn't making eye contact or budging.

Helen and I gathered up our garbage, dumped it in the trash, and moved in the direction of the steps. Guess it would be the two of us. Plus Shiner, of course, who materialized from the shadows and took up a herding position on our heels as we trooped down off the now silent porch. I backpedalled a few feet and whistled, waving as Scout's head popped up from the rear seat of the ancient Subaru. He scrambled out the open window and raced to us, his leash sailing along behind him. At the same moment, Wally's battered brown Chevy Impala came squealing off the highway from the easterly direction. Saturday morning. He must have driven Tina to her job as a tech in the only veterinarian's office in Atascadero. Wally has been on state disability for many years, but he always makes sure his wife has a full-time job. Small rocks nailed my legs as he took the corner too tight. "Ouch!" Dammit, a dog could lose an eye that way. I shook my fist, but he was paying no attention.

Helen and I started up the road. As we passed, Sunshine's beagle gave us a friendly wuff from her perch on their front porch. Approaching his driveway, we could see Dick busily hosing down the fire engine. He glanced at us once or twice, but gave no acknowledgement.

We reached the one-lane bridge spanning the steep sides of Arroyo Loco's creek, and took a moment to peer over the railing. Despite California's persistent drought, a tiny creek falls through one side of our canyon most of the year, giving minnows a place to call home in the shade of overhanging oaks. The giant trees are a popular hangout for scrub jays and crows. When the humans are quiet, the canyon echoes with the sounds of woodland songbirds, frogs, and crickets.

A faint call came from behind. Marla lumbered up the hill after us. We waited. She was breathing heavily when she caught up, and although the morning was cool, streaks of sweat ran down the sides of her face and into the heavy cleavage inside her stained sundress. No matter how cool the day, Marla was always overheated. There was a slam from the side of her house and her basenji flew out his dog door, snarling furiously at Shiner and Scout as he raced along the wire fence. Thank goodness he was securely contained.

After a second or two catching her breath, Marla narrowed her eyes and stared hard at us. "If you know what's good for you, you'll stay out of that house," she hissed. Then she turned and waddled across the road, snarling at her dog.

That was awkward. "Okay. Well," Helen whispered, "I'm beginning to wonder if Will started that fire after all." We continued climbing. Peering down Wally's long driveway, we couldn't see anything except the trees lining the drive. Wally and Tina's house is the only one built back from the road on a long driveway, and the only house that can't be seen by any other.

When we got to Helen's she ran in to get a flashlight, a hammer, and some gloves while the dogs and I stayed in the yard. Scout and Shiner are not big fans of cats, of which Helen has several, and I'm sure the cats are not fond of dogs either. We did use the opportunity to take a gander around the rear of her house, and sure enough, there was a big wire cage, maybe eight feet square, off to the side of the small patio. It was equipped with various cat perches, dishes with dried up food, and several overflowing litter boxes. The fragrance wafted toward us and we quickly retreated.

Helen was pensive upon returning. "Two questions," she said. "Really, what is it with Freda? I've seen those pictures on her walls. Is she anti-Semitic? Could she have had it in for the Rosenblums because they're Jewish?

Maybe that's why they don't get along, and never mind the magnolia."

I scanned across the canyon from Freda's front porch to Will's, and back. "I don't know, Helen. I'd hate to think so. Freda's kind of a mystery to me. I don't know anything about her really, at least from before she came here. Do you?"

"Well, you've seen that picture of The Duke, right? There must be something there."

"This place is full of mysteries," I shook my head. I was thinking about the fact that Will's nearest neighbor, and his most ardent adversary, Delia Jackson, had apparently not been home during the fire last night. There had also been no sign of her kids, sixteen-year-old DeVon or fourteen-year-old Chamise. I neglected to mention that to the deputy that morning. "So, speaking of mysteries, what kind of car does Delia drive?" Helen lives on the downhill side of Delia, so she had to know. She said it was a big, black SUV, which is sort of what I remembered. The truth is, last night as I started on my walk, I saw a small, light-colored sedan backing out of Delia's driveway. I didn't recognize the car, and it had disappeared by the time I got close. I assumed Delia or one of her kids had company. Then, when they didn't come out during all the excitement, I assumed they were gone somewhere. If they were gone, though, what was the sedan doing in their driveway when they weren't home? I decided not to share that with Helen yet.

When we got right up to Delia's house, we could see the black SUV parked in her gravel driveway uphill of the house. At that moment, the screen door slammed open. In a long, navy-blue bathrobe with matching mules, her frizzy, salt-and-pepper hair half pinned up and half flying in all directions, and with no makeup, Delia herself stormed down the broad front steps.

"What the hell happened here?" she screeched, her left arm flailing wildly in the direction of the sodden black pile of what was left of the house next door. "I go away for one day and, oh my god! Could somebody please tell me what the hell happened here?"

Helen has more sense than to try to talk to Delia when she's in one of her tirades. She backed off and put her hand on my arm. Tipping her head and rolling her eyes in the direction of Will's house, she tugged at me silently. Not wanting to be completely rude, I said, "Uh, the Rosenblums' house burned down."

"I can see the damned house burned down!" Delia screamed. Her whole face was turning a frightening shade of scarlet mixed with the usual deep brown, and a thin film of perspiration glinted in the morning sun across her forehead. "I'm not an idiot. I can see that. How did it burn down? He probably burned the damned thing down himself, didn't he?"

"Um, well, maybe," I tried again. "We don't actually know what happened."

"Oh, my god. This is shocking! A whole house burns down and nobody knows what happened? This place really is crazy!" She threw both hands wildly over her head and stormed back toward her porch, still yelling. "This place is a madhouse, a complete madhouse! It serves the old bastard right. Serves him right!" We stood there until she disappeared inside, banging the door behind her and slamming loudly out of sight.

Helen and I looked at each other. I really wanted to know where Delia had been last night, what time she left and when she returned. But now did not seem like a good time to ask those questions. We turned to continue our climb. That's when I realized Scout was no longer alongside me.

I stopped and looked around, then spotted him down in the shallow ditch that runs at the edge of the asphalt. He was sniffing and lifting his paws high as he moved around something there. Whatever it was flashed briefly in the sun, and I walked closer. From there I could see it was broken glass, so I called Scout away from it. We didn't need a sliced open paw to go with our other problems that morning.

I eased myself into the ditch to get a closer look. It was a freshly broken, one-pint Mason canning jar with the lid still screwed on the neck. Except for a rivulet of mud from last night's rain, it was clean. It must have been in the ditch only a short time. If I had to guess, I'd say the jar had broken against a rock embedded in the dirt. Someone had either thrown or dropped the closed jar down there, or maybe had fallen into the ditch while holding the jar.

"Helen," I called. "Bring me those gloves." After slipping on one of Helen's too-big gardening gloves, I carefully picked up the two largest pieces of jar: the bottom, and the piece still screwed onto the lid. I climbed carefully out of the shallow ditch. We bent our heads over the two jar pieces I cradled. Except for a wisp of white material under the lid, the jar was immaculate. Very strange.

Still carrying the pieces of broken jar, we walked past the burned house and yellow crime scene tape. The blackened ruins were silent now. Birds chirped from a lilac bush. Soft clouds drifted overhead and a gentle morning breeze shifted the ashes like the soft fur on a kitten's back.

Nature was already about her business reclaiming what the fire had destroyed. Helen and I went on to the garage where I set the jar pieces down carefully on a low rock retaining wall there alongside the building.

Helen found the loose board Randy had rotated sideways last night, but this time it wouldn't budge. We looked more closely. Ah, ha. Sometime between last night and this morning, someone had hammered a nail into the soft wood, sealing that opening. I pulled at a couple of the adjacent boards until I found another loose one, and then turned it slightly. The whole board fell off in my hands. The one next to it bent away from the frame when I tugged at it, making an opening large enough for me to lean into with the upper half of my body. Is this what they call "breaking and entering"?

There was enough light streaming through the opening I had created to see that the car was still where it had been last night. Not enough light to make out much about the dusty boxes and other objects lining the walls and scattered around the workbench. One thing that was on my mind, and the big reason I wanted to look in the garage, was that I was afraid there might be another body sitting there in the car. Sure, Janet was probably visiting her sick brother Kenneth wherever he was living. But finding that ring with the burned body last night threw many things into question. If the body was Kenneth, then where was Will? If Kenneth was dead, then Janet couldn't be visiting him. Where was she? I really did not want to flick on the flashlight and see the faces of dead people sitting in that car. Exactly like in those scary movies where the characters insist on going into the haunted house, every nerve in my body was yelling, "Don't go in there!"

I started working on making the opening larger so both Helen and I could get into the garage. If I was going to find something gruesome, I wanted company, and as I believe I've mentioned before, Helen is a big girl. Finally, we got three full boards off. Helen cranked up the eco-friendly, no-battery flashlight, and we peered around. Still very creepy. One of us should probably have stayed outside to watch in case the villain reappeared, or Deputy Muñoz, but that wasn't going to be me. I wanted to see what was in there, and I wasn't going inside by myself. Shiner was beside me and Scout was rolling around in the soft grass on the uphill side of the retaining wall, happily kicking his paws in the air. Oh, great. Probably something dead up there. Good thing we were headed for a swim at dog beach this morning. I called him down and put them both into "down-stay" guarding the opening in the garage wall. I stepped inside and pointed at them. "Watch!" I commanded. Shiner yawned and looked away. Scout perked up his ears and tried to look trustworthy. Helen followed me, holding onto my shoulder and pointing the flashlight around us. I think she was whimpering a little, but that might have been me.

"Shine the light into the car," I said, averting my gaze well to the right of the car window. If there was a body in there, Helen would see it first and scream, then I would know not to look. Who wants that image burned into memory?

"Why?" she asked. "I don't see anything in there." Only then did I remember to breathe. She stepped closer and pointed the flashlight around inside: front seat, rear seat. Nothing but a couple of recyclable grocery bags on the floorboards. The car was remarkably cleaner than mine. Of course, mine is a rolling dog crate, although that doesn't explain the discarded fast food wrappers and crumpled shopping lists littering my front seat. In any case, and more to the point, there were no bodies in Will's car, unless maybe in the trunk. I wasn't ready to look in there yet.

We started a slow shuffle around the inside of the garage, shining the light as we went and being careful not to touch anything. Some shelves with cardboard boxes on them lined part of one wall. There were a few gardening tools leaning against the far wall, and a mop bucket. Everything was dusty, and cobwebs draped from the ceiling. A dirt-encrusted window in the other side wall let in little light, and the sill was littered with dozens of dead fly bodies. Below the window was a tool bench, a few hand tools scattered on top, also very dusty and looking like they had not been used in a long time. More boxes shoved underneath and—hello, what's this? One box was pulled out, and in the light from the flashlight it was easy to see that the dust around this one had been disturbed. I reached for Helen's hand and pointed her flashlight directly at the ancient cardboard box. The flaps were torn open and I pulled one back with the tip of one still-gloved finger. Light winked at us from several clean canning jars that had been sealed in the box. I reached in and pulled one out. Sure enough, a Mason canning jar identical to the one Scout found in the ditch near Delia's house. It also still had the ring attached and there was a small box of opened lids lying beside it. An empty space gaped next to the jar I had pulled out. Okay, so someone had recently come into the garage, opened the box, and removed a jar and lid. Then somehow the jar ended up broken in the shallow ditch, but how and why?

We were feeling pretty smug about the results of our search, despite the fact that the only thing we had really accomplished was to stir up more questions. We conferred and decided to at least look down the last part of that wall before getting the heck out of there. Here is what else we found: a partially disassembled gasoline lawnmower that, judging by the fresh grass clinging to its wheels, had recently been used, a welding torch, and a half-full, rusty gas can. The dust around the gas can had not been disturbed. This made me question further the hypothesis that Will was responsible for starting the fire. Why would he go out and buy a brand new plastic gasoline can when he already had half a can of gasoline in his garage? Wouldn't he at least have used this gasoline as well, to start the fire?

By this time we were standing at the rear of the car. As good a time as any to check the trunk. Using my gloved hand, I pulled up on the latch, but it didn't budge. Helen had to use the other glove, open the driver's door, and find the latch under the dash before the trunk would pop. Guess I was feeling braver by then, because when she returned with the light, I lifted the lid. Nothing. An oil stained tire iron lay across the dirty carpet, but otherwise nothing. And no, the oil stain was not fresh blood. I started breathing again.

Then stopped. Footfalls outside the garage near the front corner. Crunching on the gravel, they came closer, more stealthily, like someone tiptoeing. The crunching sound ceased. The light streaming in the opening in the wall, our only exit, went out, a silhouette there. Not a sound from my dependable watch dogs. Helen and I were trapped with no way to escape. Where had we seen those long handled gardening tools, or anything we might use to defend ourselves? Seemed like they were all on the opposite side of the garage from where we stood. Nobody moved for a few long seconds.

"So, what are you two doing in there?" Lauren's voice penetrated the darkness in a very matter-of-fact tone.

Beside me I could feel Helen slump in relief, and we let go of each other. That's when I noticed Scout silhouetted beside Lauren, happily allowing her to scratch behind his ears. Shiner was rolling in the grass again. "Well, how did you know we were here?" Helen asked, a bit annoyed. "And how did you know it was us?"

"Ah, I was in my office upstairs and I saw you walking along and turn in here. Are you on a secret mission? And I knew you were still here because, well, you know your flashlight is still on? Anyway, what are you doing?"

I shuffled around the end of the car, then stepped out, Helen right behind me. Looking back, our tracks were visible on the dusty floor both entering and leaving the garage, not to mention circling the car. It wouldn't be hard to match those tracks to our shoes. If someone came after us, they would most certainly know we had been there. Maybe we should sweep around the tracks, or at least render them not so identifiable. Then again, that would leave fingerprints on the broom handle. Better to leave it. Half the people in town knew we were coming here anyway, and Lauren might not have been the only one to see us go inside.

As if to prove my point, just then Bryce appeared around the corner. "Oh," he said, pretending to be surprised. "You guys find anything?"

My eyes flicked to the broken jar still resting on the retaining wall where I'd left it, and I moved slightly to block it from Bryce's line of sight. The shorter this conversation, the happier I would be.

"Nope," Helen quickly replied. "Not a darn thing, Bryce."

We all stood there in awkward silence for a few seconds. Bryce stepped up on the rock wall and peered at the remains of the house. "I guess there's one good thing," he announced.

"Yeah? What's that?" Helen again. We waited while Bryce hopped down from the wall.

"A couple days ago, Will was saying he had black widow spiders all around his porch," Bryce explained. "He was afraid Janet was going to get bitten. He wanted to spray, but after that fight with Valerie and the ant poison, Delia told him she'd kill him if she saw him spraying any more bug poison. He was going to call an exterminator. Now he doesn't have to call the exterminator. I mean, all the black widows are toast."

More awkward silence. Solemnly, I shook my head and said, "Yep, guess you're right, Bryce; today is his lucky day. He sure doesn't have to call the exterminator." Silently, I wondered if maybe Will had tried to exterminate the spiders himself with his torch and accidentally started the fire that way, though that wouldn't explain the body in the bed.

Bryce nodded vacantly. "It's really Delia's lucky day too. They got into that screaming match about spraying poison, and Will was so mad he told her she wouldn't know a black widow if it bit her, and when she found them all around her house too she'd change her tune about spraying poison.

Now the spiders are dead, Delia doesn't have to worry either."

"Yep, guess you're right again, Bryce. Today is Delia's lucky day too." Helen bumped me hard from the side almost toppling me. I don't think it was an accident either, from the smirk she gave me when I righted myself enough to glance in her direction. Helen can be really funny sometimes. Other times she is a pain.

CHAPTER FIVE

Bryce walked toward the corner where he could get a better view of the piles of ashes behind the yellow crime scene tape. Suddenly a rustling erupted among the granite boulders and oaks on the rise behind the house. Dry leaves and sticks crunched and crackled, and two or maybe three teenagers took off in the other direction, shoving each other, and whispering urgently. They disappeared deeper into the underbrush as quickly as they had appeared.

"Randy! Randy, you little scamp, what are you kids doing out there?!" Bryce hollered, his face turning red, as they vanished. He shook one fist in the air angrily. "Darn kids!" Striding past us back toward the road, he stopped and turned. "And you girls better get away from here too! I've already called the sheriff's office and you're going to get into big trouble if they catch you here! This is a crime scene!" He continued angrily up canyon toward his converted garage.

"That is one strange young man," Helen observed as we watched him go. "I think he might be brain-damaged. Does he work anywhere?"

"Ah, he used to be a grocery bagger," Lauren said. "He got fired for telling the clerks how to do their jobs and insulting the customers about their food purchases. Never could get another job. He is right, though, about that fight with Delia. I was inside and couldn't hear what they were yelling about yesterday afternoon, but they were really going after each other in Delia's driveway. Screaming nose-to-nose, shaking their fists, the whole enchilada."

"Egads," I observed. "You didn't see Will with a glass jar did you?" That would be too easy.

Lauren's brow furrowed momentarily. "I don't remember a glass jar, although he was waving something around." We all turned and looked at the pieces of broken jar perched on the rock wall. "I did see him fall in the ditch, but not the jar."

"So, what have we got so far?" I sat down in the shade of the partially dismantled garage and tried to reconstruct what we had learned.

Helen put one foot on the wall and leaned on it, looking into the distance up canyon. "Okay. Well, we found a broken jar down by Delia's that obviously came from the box in the garage."

Lauren sat down on the other side of the broken pieces of jar and peered at them curiously. "What's that white stuff?" she pointed at the underside of the lid. We all leaned over and looked at it speculatively.

I picked up a thin twig and poked at the white stuff. "Definitely spider web stuff," I concluded. I was starting to get the willies. I know spiders are an important part of the web of life on earth. They still give me the willies. Was that something tickling the back of my leg? I stood up fast.

Helen summarized what we were all thinking. "Okay, Will has black widow spiders. He gets into a big fight with Delia about them. She says she won't let him spray. For some reason he comes into his garage, gets a jar, captures a couple of spiders and carries them to Delia's house. Maybe he wants to show her, to prove to her they really are black widows. Or maybe he wants to plant a few around her house. Either way, he drops the jar when he falls into the ditch, or he throws it down, or he doesn't make it all the way there before he drops it. I don't know. Something."

Lauren and I nodded. "That about sums it up," I agreed, then considered our story for a few seconds. It was still not very satisfying. "That's another can-you-believe-what-Will's-done-this-time story. I mean, we already know he does strange things. That doesn't explain why his house burned down, how a body got into the house, and it doesn't shed any light on where Janet might be now."

"Well, that's true," Helen agreed. "What do we know about that?"

"I can't believe Janet is anywhere but in the house," Lauren observed. "Will hardly ever lets her go outside."

Lauren hadn't heard about Janet's trip to see her brother. After I explained that, she still shook her head doubtfully. "Very hard to believe Will would let Janet take a trip like that by herself," she said, looking at the ground by her feet. "Some mornings I see her come out and sit on the porch steps in the sun. He's out after her within minutes and leads her inside. He doesn't let her out of his sight."

"Didn't." Helen and I spoke simultaneously.

"What?" Lauren peered at us. Then Helen explained, none too gently, about the body found among the ashes last night.

The three of us sat and stared absently at the garage wall for several more minutes. Locating Janet seemed to be the key to finding any answers. Where was Janet?

"The only way to prove Janet's not in the house, or in danger, maybe with the murderer, is to find her safely somewhere else," I started. "But nobody knows this brother

Kenneth's last name. And everything burned up with the house: address books, letters, records, everything."

"Would there be anything in the car?" Helen asked excitedly, then answered herself. "Sure, like car registration, insurance papers, who knows what else?" She headed for the opening in the garage wall, excitedly cranking the flashlight. We heard the car door creak open, and she emerged a moment later with a handful of papers. A crinkly three-year-old registration form in Will's name with their old address. That might be something, then again, probably not. A pink receipt from the Jiffy Lube in Paso Robles dated last March. The bottom half of an outdated map of California stained with coffee cup rings and what looked like dried hot dog relish stuck to Brawley and parts of the Imperial Valley. An empty flattened straw wrapper. I know sometimes we all feel like we are drowning in paper, but it's hard to think about anyone's life coming down to nothing but this handful of meaningless detritus. We shook our heads in disappointment.

That being a dead end, Helen returned the papers to the car and stowed them back in the glove compartment. I set the jar pieces inside on the floor, then Helen and I tapped the three boards into place. Anyone could still get in there any time they wanted, but I like to pick up after myself. We walked dispiritedly out to the road where I hooked Shiner on his leash. Scout was lolligagging at the corner of the garage. Helen and I waved goodbye as Lauren crossed to her place.

As soon as she was out of ear shot, Helen tipped her head to mine. "Okay, what about Valerie? She really hates Will, and they're right across the road. She could have easily run over here last night, started the fire, and run home."

"Lauren would know," I answered. "You think Lauren's faking innocence? Valerie would have to run right between Freda's and Delia's, or your place, to get there. That's too many potential witnesses. She'd have to be carrying a bright red plastic gas can too, remember. No, it would be more likely to be someone on Will's side of the canyon coming in from the rear."

"Well, I still think there's something wrong with that Valerie. The way she either whispers all sickly sweet or else screams instead of talking. And her moods. Sheesh, she's like a jack-in-the-box with those moods. She's always angry. I think she must be brain-damaged or something." Helen paused. "Someone from Will's side of the canyon, coming in from the rear? Like you, you mean?" I couldn't tell if she was serious. She punched me gently on the arm and continued. "Well, anyway, maybe that's why Lauren is hanging out with us. She wants to know what we know, or suspect."

Except for the brain-damaged part, Helen made a good point. "Hmm. Yeah, let's keep Valerie on the list," I agreed. We started back down canyon.

"You know," I said, thinking out loud, "I'd kind of like to check out that place where the kids were hanging out."

"What do you think you might find?"

I stopped and looked up in that direction. "I don't know. I don't like the idea of kids out under those oaks. They're probably smoking and who knows what else."

Helen took a couple more steps, then stopped and looked back too. "Well, good luck with that. Whatever they're doing up there, we can't stop them, and I don't want them getting pissed off at me and setting my house on fire too."

I considered this possibility. "So you think that's what happened? You think the kids set the fire?" I wasn't convinced.

She looked at the ground in front of her, then shook her head. "Okay, no, I guess I don't think that. Whoever started that fire did it deliberately, and planned it well in advance, buying gas and all. It wasn't a badly aimed cigarette. No, I don't think the kids started the fire." She started off again, then stopped. "Okay. Well, according to what Bryce said, Delia threatened to kill Will the afternoon before he died. You think Delia did it?"

"Hmm. Yeah, she does have a fiery personality." Helen cut me a sideways glance.

We walked together as far as her driveway, where we said goodbye. I called Scout to catch up, attached his leash, and allowed myself to be dragged the rest of the way. I wish someone could explain to me why a dog walking off leash will always lag behind, while one walking on leash will invariably pull ahead.

As we crossed the single-lane bridge spanning the creek, Scout gave a startled bark and peered into the shadows underneath. I too leaned over one side. We heard stumbling steps and urgent whispers and the same three teenage boys took off from under the other side of the bridge. About fifty feet up stream they quickly climbed the bank of the creek, their sneakers slipping in the slick clay from last night's rain, and disappeared through the underbrush there.

I dashed to that side and could see a thin trail cutting up the creek bank in the direction they had vanished.

Looking down, sure enough, there was a trail running alongside the creek, almost invisible under the branches overhanging the water. I've lived in Arroyo Loco almost four years, and I never knew there was a trail down there. As the dogs and I went on to the car, I considered this interesting development. The trail must run behind Will's house because that's the way the kids had come, probably past Delia's, Helen's, Wally and Tina's, then along through the creek bed, under the bridge and maybe continuing behind the houses on the other side of the road. Who knows how much more extensive the trail system might be? I thought about all the belongings that had gone missing through the years from folks' rear porches. Maybe the trail went up behind my house farther up canyon as well. As the dogs and I climbed into the car, I resolved to explore that trail myself when we returned this afternoon.

Lost in thought, I drove the winding two-lane highway toward Morro Bay. If the body found in the fire was not Will, then where was he? Wherever he was, he didn't take his car. Might he be hiding in the canyon behind our houses? Randy and the other kids had been roaming that canyon since they were little and probably had any number of hideouts where a man could take refuge for at least a few days. Whoever set that fire clearly didn't care if the rest of the houses at our end of the canyon went up in smoke too. They may have intended for that to happen, and the plan was only foiled by a well-timed rain shower. What was there to stop them from trying again? I thought about my cozy home, and what my dogs and I would do if a raging wildfire came at us from down canyon. We could run, but we would be trapped at the end of the road. I shuddered.

As soon as I returned home, I would come up with an alternative escape plan in case of such emergency.

My car came out of the last series of downhill switchbacks, around the last curve, and suddenly the long coast opened out in front of us. Giant Morro Rock took center stage, rising more than fifty stories above the surrounding shining flat beaches. In the brilliant sunshine, the dark folds and crevices of the rock contrasted boldly with exposed surfaces whitewashed with gull droppings. The ocean was a deep blue-purple that morning, reflecting the now cloudless sky. I swung the car north on Highway 1, the last motels of Morro Bay whizzing past on our right. A few miles north of town, I slowed where the median ended, then turned quickly left across two lanes of southbound traffic and bumped off the pavement onto the weedy potholed, narrow shoulder of the highway. The car came to a stop nosed up close to a rusty cyclone fence at the edge of the beach. A few other cars were wedged in alongside us at various angles, meaning Scout and Shiner would have playmates for their romp on the beach. I got them out the side door, holding tightly to their leashes, and we stepped through a large opening cut through the rusting fence. It has never been entirely clear that humans are permitted on this beach, let alone off-leash dogs. On the other hand, there's a roll of plastic bags tied to the fence for use in cleaning up after the dogs, and someone regularly picks up the trash from the battered oil drum sitting by the opening. It's one of those situations where it's probably best to apologize later rather than ask permission first.

The dogs pointed their noses into the air, their mouths slightly open as they breathed deeply of the cool, salty wind. Shiner stood still while his sensitive nose gathered information. Then, suddenly, he bounded off down the beach, long fur streaming, and young muscles pulling his lithe body in a black-and-white streak across the sand. Scout followed close on his heels. I know what the folks at Disneyland say, but I have always contended that the only genuinely "happiest place on Earth" is any place where a well-loved healthy dog can run safely and freely.

Far down the beach, a small reddish-brown four-legged creature stopped, turned, then came racing in our direction. It was Jax, a young golden retriever and my dogs' best beach friend. They all ran directly toward one another, like a dog version of that sappy romantic advertisement. When they got close, all three tails started gyrating madly, and then, standing on hind legs, they took turns throwing their forelegs around one another and play-bowing in the sand. In a flurry of wildly happy barks, they turned and began a series of wide looping circles between Jax's human companion, almost out of sight at the other end of the beach, and myself.

I walked slowly north as the dogs played. I could feel my neck and shoulders relaxing, my breath deepening, and my mind clearing. Farther north, at Piedras Blancas Lighthouse near San Simeon, the waves crash and boom into rocks and crumbling cliffs, but along this quiet stretch of beach south of Cayucos, the waves are more pacific, rolling gently onto the sand, then hissing as they pull back out to sea. The rhythm calmed my fears and concerns. I walked on as though in meditation.

Slowly, the picture came to me of a tall, old man lying peacefully in an ancient iron bedstead as the room around him flamed then turned to ashes. Something about that picture did not make sense. It is sadly true that people can and do get trapped in burning buildings and lose their lives. They get trapped in prisons of their own creation when they install bars on their windows or when they put deadbolts on doors and can't get to the key. They get trapped when they try to stand up and walk out of a burning house instead of staying close to the floor, or when they open a door to flames and are overcome by the exploding fire. They are trapped by smoke, fumes, and fire when they go back inside to rescue a child or a beloved pet. We've all seen those safety videos and public service messages dozens of times. But none of those things happened to the tall man. He stayed there as the fire consumed the house, the bedding on which he was lying, and eventually, his body as well. That's what didn't make sense. Why didn't he try to get out?

Perhaps he wanted to die, although it's hard to imagine being able to lie still while that was happening. Maybe he had taken sleeping pills or some other drug and was unable to react. It's also possible he was dead before the fire started. If the body was really that of Janet's gravely ill brother, maybe he died of natural causes. In that case, the fire was more of a funeral pyre than a means of death.

The dogs made a final run around me and then trotted off together to begin a sniffing exploration of the logs, trash, and dead things deposited on the beach by the last high tide. It was only a matter of time before one of them found something delicious to roll in. Time to pull the carefully hidden Chuckit out of my beach bag and engage them in some supervised tennis ball chasing and swimming. We played that way for another half hour. When they had all gotten as drenched with salt water as possible, covered with as many pounds of sand as their bedraggled coats could carry, and had decorated themselves and each other with bits of dead seaweed and globs of dog slobber, I stowed the toys in my bag and turned around. I waved at Jax's owner, still far down the beach. After looking back wistfully two or three times, Shiner and Scout reluctantly left their companion and trailed after me. I tried not to watch as my sandy, wet dogs hopped into the back of the old Subaru. I have heard that trying to keep a car clean when you have dogs is like trying to brush your teeth while eating Oreos. No argument here. In our pack, I've caved on the keeping-the-car-clean thing. The backseat is theirs.

On the outskirts of Morro Bay, we swung into the Piggly Wiggly shopping center and stopped at Pacito's ramshackle taqueria for a couple of take-out, grilled fish tacos and a side of refried beans. The warmth and fragrance of meat sizzling and chili simmering washed over me when I pulled open the door. As usual, I was dieting, so I skipped the Mexican rice and soda. Wisps of afternoon fog were beginning to drift back in by then. I ate my meal sitting in the car in the oil-stained parking lot. As usual, the tacos were superb. With fire-grilled white fish, crunchy cabbage, and freshly made salsa, they were practically health food. I licked the last juices from my fingers and returned to the taqueria for a small chocolate shake for dessert. I don't want to give the impression that I order the milkshake on a regular basis, but Pacito's wife did have it already made for me when I popped back in.

It was after three o'clock by the time we rolled up to the roadhouse, and everything seemed quiet. The mail carrier had already completed her appointed rounds. Sunshine in her black stretchy yoga leotard and long, rainbow broom skirt was swishing toward the set of metal mailboxes. I waved and pulled the car to a stop. It's strictly forbidden to park there, but I was only going to be a second. I'd been wanting to get Sunshine's private thoughts on the fire and events of the night before. Seemed like the perfect opportunity

"Hey, Sunshine," I called as I joined her. "How are you today?"

"Oh," she sighed, dragging her silver ponytail across one shoulder and stroking it lovingly. "My tummy's been bothering me, and my innards are all upset. I think I need to go on another meditation retreat."

I furrowed my brow and gave her my best concerned-psychotherapist expression. She turned her dark eyes toward mine. Sunshine has eyes that look like Bambi's mother's eyes would look if she hadn't been shot. Although Sunshine often seems sad, I've never seen her cry. This time, tears threatened to spill. That psychotherapist look, sort of a cross between a lost puppy and that all-compassionate mother for whom most of us are still waiting, does sometimes bring out the tears. She looked into the distance. "Why does there have to be all this ugliness?" she sighed. "Why can't we all get along? Why can't we be nice to each other?"

I didn't have an answer for her, so I gently patted her shoulder. She gave another deep shuddering sigh. The scent of herbal soap drifted upward, along with her ever-present patchouli.

"There's this other thing." She paused. I waited. "I'm afraid this might be all my fault," she finally said.

"What are you talking about?"

"Janet being missing, maybe the house burning down, and that body..." she shuddered again.

I held her shoulders. "What does any of that have to do with you? What do you mean, it might be your fault?"

She looked away for a second and tucked a loose strand behind an ear. "Janet has a sad angel's soul, and Will trusts me. I stay with her when he goes for groceries and we visit. Janet doesn't have dementia. She's painfully sad. Her spirit is anguished. Will loves her with all his heart. That's why he controls her. It was his dream for them to move here and live in peace and fulfillment. She misses her family and friends, her activities, her life. When she got this message that her brother was sick, she wanted to go see him. Will was against it. He was afraid for her. So I told him I would go with her. She assured me it'd be okay. Alice and I picked her up and took her to the bus station." Sunshine sighed deeply. "If Janet had stayed home, I don't think any of the rest of this would've happened. Now we don't know where she is, her house is gone, and Will might be... gone too." Sunshine fell gently against my shoulder and I put my arms around her. "Why don't I just mind my own business?" she murmured.

"You can't have known all of this was going to happen. She told you she would be fine. What you did makes sense to me," I tried to reassure her. "We all thought she had dementia." I guess that's what we always assume whenever an older person acts depressed and withdrawn.

Sunshine stood straighter and gazed off across the highway. "I don't know. Maybe she behaves that way to avoid those horrible arguments with Will and to keep him from pestering her so much. If we think he's hard to live around, imagine having to live in the same house with him."

"Yeah," I considered that. "That must be hellish."

Only then did we turn toward the long bank of mailboxes. Simultaneously, we opened our respective boxes and began to extract the contents. Let's see, three junk mails and a Netcast bill. What, are they billing me twice a month now? I swear I paid this last week!

"That's odd," Sunshine said quietly looking down at a medium-sized brown envelope in her hand.

"What's that?"

"I don't know. There's no address on it, or postage. My name's not on it." She turned it over a couple of times, then handed me the envelope, which was slightly crushed from having been pushed through the too-small mailbox opening. It was sealed tightly, had no writing on it at all, and I could feel a small stack of index-sized cards inside.

"Should we open it?" she puzzled. "It's too small to be a bomb, right?"

What? Who assumes a blank envelope arriving unexpectedly contains a bomb? People are so strange sometimes. Not that I'm complaining. At my house, human frailties pay the bills. In any case, I'm no expert on explosive devices. "No, I don't think it could be a bomb." I returned it to her, deciding not to say anything about anthrax.

Betsy Carper's freckled face appeared at the steps. Why did Betsy always seem to be lurking around somewhere nearby? "Hi, girls!" she called out lightly as she bounced up, and added, "What's not a bomb?"

Suddenly, Delia's voice boomed as she clumped around the corner of the porch in thick-soled clogs. "A bomb! Oh, my god! Will's house was bombed?" Delia's loud arrival reminded me why it's no wonder no one can have much of a private life in Arroyo Loco, and how rumors get started here. Now poured overabundantly into a bright-red, Lycra exercise outfit, her hair carefully caught up on top in a matching red Scrunchie, Delia rushed towards us, her musky perfume arriving first. Still looking puzzled, Sunshine waved the envelope a little, and Delia eagerly snatched it away from her. Her disappointment was obvious. "This isn't a bomb. What are you giving me this for?"

Four of us were now on the porch, all trying to get a better look at the plain, brown envelope. I explained how Sunshine found it stuffed in her mailbox. Before I could finish, Delia thrust a corner into her mouth and ripped it open with her teeth, getting red lipstick on the edge. Hmm. What if there really was anthrax in there? Would I be sad? What if that envelope and its contents were important evidence? Delia reached inside and extracted a few well-thumbed black and white photographs, pulling them close to study. A small piece of note paper fluttered to the porch floor, and I picked it up before leaning in to peer at the top photograph. Betsy hopped up and down beside Delia, trying to get a better look from her angle.

From what I could see it was a picture of vegetation, as though the shot was taken through tree branches. I could make out a figure in the background. No, two figures. Wally was the one facing toward the camera and it looked like he was standing on his own porch. The other, smaller figure had long, dark hair flowing down her back. I didn't recognize her from that angle, but if I had to guess I would say she looked like… . Delia flipped to the next photograph.

This one was taken from several feet closer and at a slightly different angle. Both figures could be seen from the side in this shot, and yes, the girl was definitely twelve-year-old Sofia. Sofia and her mother Graciela live at the corner of Arroyo Loco and the highway, directly across from where we stood. Graciela runs her real estate business out of an office tacked onto the front of the small house. I glanced up and could see her signboard propped out there now, indicating that her office was open and she was within. I looked back at the photographs in time to see the third shot, either taken from close up or with one of those fancy telephoto lenses. In that shot, Wally was stroking the neckline of Sofia's low scoop-neck tank top with the long stem of a native California drought-tolerant grass. The stem looked like one that had been plucked from the bed bordering Wally's porch. The photograph caught the leering smile on his face as he gazed at Sofia's neckline. My stomach lurched with nausea.

"What the hell?" Delia whispered quietly and flipped to the next photograph. Overcome with frustration, Betsy grabbed at the photographs and pulled them down to where she could see them, but Delia wasn't letting go.

"This is disgusting!" Betsy said, "He's got his hand in her shirt!"

I was feeling kind of wobbly by then, and Sunshine had turned a strange shade of grayish-green. I took her arm and we both sat down on the bench by the railing. There were a couple more photographs, but I didn't want to see them. Hearing Betsy moaning, "Oh, my god," as she looked was enough for me.

Staring at the pictures, Delia shook her head slowly back and forth, her face turning that odd shade of scarlet again, her heavily made-up lips pressed tightly together. I couldn't remember ever before seeing Delia with nothing to say. Still without speaking, she shoved the photographs into the envelope and raised it deliberately in the air. "These are going straight to the sheriff," she snarled, her voice tight and hard. "Straight to the sheriff, and I'm taking them myself right this minute." She stormed angrily down the porch steps still waving the envelope, and then turned back toward us. "But first, I'm going to shoot that bastard in the head and then I'll blow his balls off! Or maybe the other way around."

Betsy was the first to react, rushing down the steps and running after Delia. "No, no, Delia! Don't do that! Let me handle it! Wally will listen to me! I'm an expert in difficult communications. Let me talk to him. I know I can persuade him to confess everything and turn himself in to the sheriff." She jogged alongside the much taller woman, tugging at her red Lycra sleeve, trying in vain to slow her down.

Damn. I really wanted to ask Delia about that sedan in her driveway last night. On the other hand, interrupting her on her mission to shoot Wally didn't seem like the right time to be asking potentially impertinent questions, especially since I was in full support of her mission. Guess I'd have to wait.

CHAPTER SIX

About that time, I remembered the slip of paper in my hand. It was pale blue, torn from a small spiral-bound notebook. The words written on it were scrawled in the crabbed handwriting of an old person. All it said was, "a word to the wise," and it was not signed. Someone put those photographs into that envelope, added the note, and stuffed the package into Sunshine's mailbox. Was Sunshine's box chosen at random, or was there some significance to that choice? Among the residents of Arroyo Loco, Sunshine was probably the most likely to try to sweep difficult issues under the rug and to pretend everything was fine. So the placement of the note and photographs into her mailbox didn't seem to make much sense. Then again, not everyone knew Sunshine the way I did, and maybe the person who delivered the envelope had a different impression of her.

Next to me, Sunshine gave another deep sigh. "Sunshine," I asked, "do you have any idea who might have put those photographs in your mailbox, or why they would have chosen to put them in your box?"

She didn't seem to want to make eye contact, her gaze shifting from her lap to the distance and back again. Finally, after several more seconds of silence, she whispered, "I thought you put them there, Estela." I was too stunned to say anything at all. Then she went on. "You're the one who's been complaining about Wally hanging out with the little girls, and about how no one will listen to you. You're a psychologist. You always assume the worst about people. I think you took the photographs. I think you're trying to stir up trouble around here." The silence hung between us. "Are you telling me you didn't take those pictures and put them in my mailbox?"

Still stunned, it was hard for me to formulate an answer. What had happened to Sunshine's usual sunny disposition? "No, I did not take those pictures, Sunshine. No, I did not put them in your mailbox." So far, so good. "Yes, I have seen Wally behaving in ways that I felt were inappropriate. Like that time he was riding Randy's little sister around on his shoulders, holding her thighs and snuggling his head in her crotch, and I told you about that. You said I was imagining things, that he just likes to play with the girls."

Her eyes brimming again with unshed tears, Sunshine gave a noncommittal, "Humph," and looked away. "I still think it was you," she said quietly. She stood, and slowly started to ease away.

The problem with going through life believing that wanting something to be true will make it true is that it won't. Likewise, pretending that something is not there doesn't make it go away. And while one is busy wishing and pretending, actions that might really help are not being taken. I had nothing to do with those photographs, but increasingly it seemed like the only way to clear my name was going to be to find out who was responsible for whatever was going on in Arroyo Loco.

"Sunshine, please!" I entreated. "I didn't take those pictures, and I'm not trying to stir up trouble around here!

But you saw it yourself! There is trouble here, and pretending it's not here won't make it go away. What's worse, that's not fair to the little girls Wally is molesting. Obviously, someone other than me is noticing now. You saw the pictures."

Abruptly, Amanita appeared at the bottom of the steps, almost like she had been sneaking up on us. "Whose car is this?" she immediately demanded. "Parking is not allowed here!" She pointed accusingly at the offending vehicle. "I'm going to speak to the HOA parking police and make sure they enforce our community rules, otherwise people will park wherever they want whenever they want, destroying the serenity of our beautiful community! Some people are so inconsiderate of others!"

Oh, geez. There were parking police in Arroyo Loco? In all fairness to Amanita, if she hadn't been the one pointing out my sins, it would have been someone else. There's always someone around to scold a rule breaker. Will, for example, had a talent for showing up and calling attention whenever a violation occurred. Except Will wouldn't usually yell. He would, "accidentally" trip, fall against an offensively parked vehicle with some small tool, and leave a gouge in the paint. Exactly like the one visible on the hood of my car that day. I had pulled over in front of his house once, only for a minute to drop some misdirected mail at Freda's, and I came out to find that gouge. Bryce was another one who would show up to snarl, or maybe Betsy would suddenly rematerialize, scolding the driver, the car, and the dogs.

I glared at Amanita as I started toward my car. It was obvious the Subaru was mine, since both border collies had their heads out the rear window closest to Amanita. A low growl began to grumble in Shiner's throat, and he lifted one side of his upper lip. I was tempted to let the situation develop further, but Amanita started screeching about vicious dogs and threatening to call animal control, so I went on down and slipped into the driver's seat. In the meantime, Sunshine had escaped quickly off toward her house. With a feeling of deep sadness, I watched her go.

I was about to turn on the ignition when I remembered about Graciela being in her office. The photographs showed Wally with her little girl. Someone should tell her. If it had been my daughter, I would want to be told. On the other hand, if people were going to blame the messenger, as it seemed they usually did, I was feeling reluctant to be the bearer of more bad news. I started to take my key out of the ignition, then saw Sunshine stop and look in the direction of the real estate office. Slowly, she turned and started that way, glancing at me as she passed. Good for you, Sunshine, I thought, as she headed to Graciela's door, her head bowed, but her feet moving forward.

A reedy whine accosted me from the porch railing above, "What pictures?" Amanita must have been eavesdropping as we stood looking at the photographs. Only then did I realize that both Sunshine and I had completely ignored Amanita and walked off in the middle of her tirade without a word. No wonder she goes out of her way to make our lives difficult. Without remorse, I continued to pretend not to hear her as I started up the car and headed home.

By the time I pulled up to my screened porch, the dogs were rested from their nap in the car and ready for another run. I put them inside the rusting wire fence. It was still only three thirty by the kitchen clock. Plenty of daylight left to explore that trail the kids were using behind Will's house this morning. Maybe I could also hike up canyon to scope out an escape route should a fire ever trap us at home. I sat down at the kitchen table and gazed out at the oaks. What would I be looking for if I went along that hidden trail?

Janet was still missing, although maybe at her brother's house, wherever that was located. Only one body had been found, so one or both of the others could be out there hiding along the trail. The red, plastic gas can had been found in that direction, so there might be some additional evidence if I kept my eyes open. There had been a fire, but also a death; maybe there would be some clues about how that happened. There might be a dangerous arsonist and murderer lurking out there.

I peered further out at the hillside behind my house, searching for some sign of a trail. Too bad I couldn't start hiking from here. I'd explored that area before and had never seen a trail, only a few hunks of granite to sit on in the sun. There was also plenty of poison oak, and more than a few rattlesnakes. Going to the closet, I changed into jeans and got out my small day pack and lightweight hiking boots. Thinking again about the snakes, I exchanged the lighter boots for heavy leather ones, added an extra layer of wool socks, and carefully tucked the hems of my jeans into the socks. I double-checked that my first aid kit, signal whistle, extra dog leash, and an old tennis ball still lived in the day pack. After filling a small water bottle, I stuffed in a crank-up flashlight, a pocketknife, and a couple of plastic bags for evidence. A bug-repellant long-sleeved shirt and my beloved Giants baseball cap completed the ensemble. I considered, then discarded the idea of packing a sandwich. After all, I was only going to be walking along a trail behind my house for twenty minutes or so. Starving to death was not likely in that time. Still, a couple of Fig Newtons wouldn't hurt. I tucked two of them in one of the small plastic evidence bags.

What with the snakes and poison oak, I really didn't want to take the dogs. Dogs don't get poison oak, but they do get the oil on their coats, and they love to share when we get home. They are also likely to get bitten if they meet a rattlesnake face-to-face. Considering that reminded me about the time Nina and I saw a mountain lion while lounging on her rear deck sucking up margaritas. Both of us are equally certain she wasn't a figment of our alcohol-impaired imaginations. She sat there looking at the house and at us, then got up and casually strolled into the underbrush. Since I would prefer the dogs not meet any mountain lions, taking them along seemed like an increasingly bad idea. At the same time, I didn't want to be out there by myself. This time though, I was going to have to go alone. I wouldn't risk my guys.

Convincing them they couldn't come along was the problem. Although they were always fine when I drove away, if I walked away from the house without taking them, Scout could be counted on to dismantle the house while I was gone, including shredding drapes, carpets, and random upholstery. Shiner would howl mournfully and inconsolably. I decided to drive as far as Will's house and park there. At least I could find the trail from that point, and if something happened to me, and I didn't make it back, eventually someone would notice the car and come looking for me. Maybe.

Almost immediately, I found the place behind Will's house where the kids were sitting this morning. It was a small clearing surrounded by chunks of granite and covered by the lower limbs of several oaks. I climbed onto one of the larger rocks and looked down over Arroyo Loco. Will's backyard and what was left of the house were directly below. Interesting. Will had an outlawed lawn behind his house. It was nicely mowed too. Over the top of his garage I could see the side and rear porch on Freda's little bungalow and the upstairs windows at Valerie and Lauren's. The backyard and side windows of Delia's house were in clear view, including a bedroom windows upstairs. I climbed down and peered through where a few smaller rocks and some short bushes made me invisible from any of the houses.

The dirt of the clearing floor was swept clean of fallen leaves and looked well-trodden. There were other signs of frequent and recent habitation. Fresh cigarette butts filled a chipped ceramic plate tucked under the overhang of one rock. The kids were definitely smoking here, but at least they disposed of their butts in a safe and environmentally friendly manner. The corner of a clear plastic bag peeked out from a nook between two rocks. I gingerly pulled at the corner, and out tumbled the bag, filled to the brim with smashed aluminum cans. It reeked of stale beer. Yes, they were drinking here, which they should not be doing. On the other hand, they were planning to recycle their empty cans. They got points for that.

I sat down on a rock to think things over. Those Fig Newtons were gnawing away at the edge of my thoughts and distracting my powers of deduction, so I dug them out of the day pack and ate them, not so much because I was hungry, but because I needed the bag to stow a few of the cigarette butts. Those were evidence, right? I'd have to be sure to remember to explain the cookie crumbs mixed in with the butts if they did turn out to be important later.

The kids do smoke up here, and the house below went up in flames last night. There's at least a reasonable possibility that a casually tossed cigarette butt may have sparked that blaze. I squeezed between the rocks again toward Will's backyard and flicked one of the cold dead butts as far I as could in that direction. It landed in the weeds about two feet in front of me, and far from any possible point of ignition for last night's fire. It landed so close to me that I reached out and retrieved it. No sense in leaving confusing evidence around.

Then I climbed onto the largest boulder and tried again. This time the butt arced out, but then dropped sharply and fell into the weeds about six feet out, still short of the lawn. I tried a few more to see what would happen, but had no more success than with the first couple. It was possible that weather conditions were impeding the flight of my experimental butts, or that my butt-flicking skills had declined appreciably since the height of my own teenage efforts. Maybe boys were better at this than girls, or maybe lit cigarettes flew better than dampish dead ones. In any case, if the fire was ignited by a lighted cigarette butt, it seemed unlikely the butt had been tossed from up here in the clearing or from the rocks surrounding it.

I climbed down and stepped as carefully as I could through the already trampled weeds, picking up the butts I had flicked. This must have been about where Ernie and Dick found the plastic gas can. From here the clearing was still well hidden behind the granite and brush. What a great place the kids had to spy on the activities in this middle part of Arroyo Loco.

I returned to the clearing and after a few false starts, found where the trail took off downhill from this gathering place. It was a narrow trail, almost like a deer trail, which I considered maybe is how it started life. The damp dirt was well enough packed that only faint sneaker prints were visible. Every so often I could see the edge of a deer hoof. Brush and small trees continued to hide my presence from the houses below. The trail skirted Will's yard, then curved out and wide around the rear of Delia's two-story. In passing, I noticed a small spur heading off toward her house. The brush had grown low across the spur. A person would have to belly-crawl through to find what could be seen in that direction. Briefly, I considered the possibility, but discretion being the better part of valor, not to mention the ground was still muddy, I decided against that. How embarrassing would it be to be found crawling around in the bushes like some demented teenager? Still, it did look suspiciously like that spur went to a place where it would have a splendid view into the undraped rear windows of the house occupied by Delia, DeVon, and Chamise.

The canyon, and the trail with it, took a sharp dip as it passed behind Helen's house. A more obvious spur took off in the direction of her backyard. I stayed on the main trail as it climbed slightly behind Wally and Tina's, giving that house a wide berth, and then dropped quickly into the bed of the small creek. Now within view of the narrow banks of the creek, I could see the trail threading through reeds as it disappeared into the bed of the creek itself, still running with silt and water from last night's rain. Upstream, a hundred feet or so from where I was standing now, was where the kids had burst from under the bridge that morning and slipped up the muddy embankment. I could pick the trail up there at another time, and save myself the trouble of wading through that soggy creek bed. Turning, I returned the way I had come down.

Meandering my way up, I decided to explore the spur trail behind Helen's backyard. Crouching down to duck under some brush, I came out where the spur ended behind a few granite rocks. I stayed low and peeped over one. Yup, Helen's backyard all right. The wire cat cage was slightly below me and directly in front about thirty feet. There did not appear to be any occupants in the cage this afternoon.

Ducking down, I scrambled up to peer over the other rock. Hello, what's this? I was looking at Wally's front porch, slightly from the side. A totally creeped out feeling crawled along my spine as I realized that I was sitting in the exact spot from where those photographs of Wally messing with Sofia had been taken. Someone who knew this trail and who knew what Wally was up to had come right here and taken those photographs. Without moving, I looked carefully around the ground, under the bushes, around the rocks, but could see no evidence of the prior presence of any other person. On the other hand, it began to dawn on me, I probably was leaving plenty of evidence of my being here. Bits of fabric, traces of dead hair and skin, DNA all around. No crime scene lab tech worth her salt would have any trouble establishing my presence at the site where those photographs were taken. Most likely, given the proclivities of Arroyo Loco's numerous residents, I was being observed at this exact moment. I looked out suspiciously at the houses I could see: Wally's, Helen's, the front corner of Delia's, Thomas's roof across the road, the upstairs of Valerie and Lauren's, and, I realized with a start, the front window of Marla's house staring directly back at me.

I slithered slowly to the base of the rock. Sitting there in the damp dirt, I focused on the arch formed by dry brush in the direction of the main trail. Concentrating and looking around, I could see several places where tiny branches were broken off at about three feet. I hadn't broken those. I inspected a couple of the broken ends up close, like one of those television detectives. From my careful scrutiny, it did seem those broken ends were wet, meaning they had been broken before last night's rain. So some person or persons about three feet tall, or a much taller person who could scrunch down to that height, had hunched along this spur, settled here, and taken those photographs of Wally. That part was obvious. Not so clear was how this information could be shared with anyone without thoroughly incriminating myself.

Scrambling back out to the main trail, I stood up. What the kids had here was a secret route to travel up and down the canyon through Arroyo Loco without much likelihood of being observed by any of the residents. Apparently, in addition to this main trail, there were spurs along it providing observation points for each house and access into each yard along the way. Anyone walking along this trail could see into these houses. I shivered, and not because of the fog that was now settling into the lower canyon. Was someone watching me now?

I wondered if my own house could be observed from this trail. Naive to think it couldn't. Being of a somewhat suspicious nature myself, and maybe a little fearful, I always close my drapes at night, but many residents of Arroyo Loco do not. Especially not on the rear windows, which look out onto the oaks. I was more than a little curious to know if my house and yard could be seen from this trail. With an anxious shudder, I started back toward the clearing behind Will's house.

Once there, I poked around until the trail going on uphill revealed itself. It went steeply at first and crested the ridge somewhere between my house and Will's. From there, it dropped sharply under heavy tree cover on the west side of the ridge. Between the incoming fog and the thick trees overhead, the darkness felt almost like nightfall. I couldn't shake the feeling I was being watched. A thunderous rustle in the underbrush at trail's edge, and I jumped, falling backward, my heart pounding. Settling into a seated position, I stared with wide eyes at the place, but nothing was moving. It is sometimes amazing how much noise one little sparrow can make in dry brush. Still, since I was already down there, I dug around in my pack, dragged out the flashlight and began to crank it up. The grinding nearly stopped me. The sound was announcing my position to anyone or anything within several dozen yards. I couldn't think about that. It was dark along there!

The light aimed where I'd heard the noise revealed nothing. The rustle had been a lizard or a small bird, or something equally as terrifying. As long as the light was already on, I looked up the trail, ahead where it disappeared around a giant boulder. Nothing could be seen beyond the rock. I stopped moving and listened. I could have sworn I heard someone breathing. What if the murderer was still lurking up here? Should I go forward around the boulder to see whatever was behind it, or should I panic, run, and stumble down the trail and out to the safety of my cozy little Subaru? I took a deep, slow, calming breath. At this point, the trail was only a few hundred yards from my own house, up over the ridge. I really did want to see what the trail was like up there. If I got that far, and had access to my yard, maybe I would pick up Scout and Shiner after all and have their company to protect me for the rest of the exploration. With knees shaking, I crept stealthily toward the boulder.

Peering around the edge, I could see there were two boulders fallen together, maybe twenty feet tall. The space between them formed an opening like a triangular cave. The cave was wide enough to accommodate a person, and it was dark enough and deep enough that I couldn't see to the end of it. Should I crank up the light again and look in there? Who might be hiding in that darkened opening? A murderer? An arsonist? A hoodlum teenager bent on evil?

Stepping back, I thought about turning tail, but knew the terror of something coming up behind would overwhelm me. After another deep breath, I realized that was a perfect opportunity to practice those assertiveness skills I had been meaning to work on for years.

With a final, cleansing yoga breath, I stepped around the boulder and began cranking up the flashlight. Whirrrr, whirrr, whirrr. That should be enough. Opening my eyes wide, I stared intently at the shadows under the giant rocks. My thumb squarely on the switch, ready to flick it on, I raised the flashlight and aimed it straight into the opening. My last thought was that the flashlight would make a great weapon with which to conk an attacker over the head, if one were needed. My thumb moved forward and flicked the switch.

Eeeoow! Eeeoow! Eeeoow! Eeeoow!

Damn! I'd hit the siren switch instead of the light! Damn! I flicked it off and turned the flashlight around, feeling around for the other switch, the one that worked the light. Found it. Flick, flash! Right into my eyes. Damn it all! I turned the light toward the cave, but couldn't see anything because I'd half blinded myself with the light.

At that point, the element-of-surprise thing was probably blown. At least my fear level was somewhat decreased. I was more pissed off and exasperated than scared. I let my eyes adjust. As far as I could see, there was definitely no one in that cave. I took a step forward. A small fire pit had been hollowed out in the dirt under the overhang of the rocks. I took a closer look. Half-hidden in the shadows were a couple of empty cans of chili, one partly filled with dirt and more cigarette butts. Hey, wait a second. Those cans were my brand of chili. I knew I had more chili than was there last time I went looking for it in the pantry on my porch. Those darn kids. Or whoever. Standing up straighter, I slowly panned the flashlight 360 degrees around me. The shadows of trees and branches moved eerily as the light passed, but other than that, nothing was visible.

Wait. What was that on the ground under the shadow of the rock overhang? I peered at the dusty ground about fifteen feet outside the cave's entrance. Was that a dead animal or maybe a bloody body part? When I pointed the fading light in that direction, the lump did not move. I eased that way, stopping to pick up a twig. I cranked up the light again, keeping my gaze on the inert lump. As I got close I could see it was probably nothing. I poked at it, then hooked it on the end of my stick and raised it up for a good look. Hmm. Kind of reddish, a ratty, old, faded 49ers sweatshirt with the sleeves cut off. Humph. Well, at least that wasn't mine. Dropping it to the ground, I looked around one last time. There weren't any interesting clues to collect here. Except for the chili cans and sweatshirt, the place was clean.

I considered the possibility of taking a closer look inside that shadowy cave. A person would have to crawl and wedge themselves in between those rocks to get there. Probably a bad idea. Assertiveness is one thing; going out of one's way to find trouble is another.

With one last look around, I located the place where the trail continued. I moved, and there was that rustling again, uphill and to my left. Only this time it was more of a crunch. Not even the most overweight lizard is going to make that loud of a crunch. I started walking again, listening with each step. The trail rose, crossed back over the ridge and brightened as it emerged from under the deep tree cover. More crunching. I stared hard in the direction of the sound. Like those grainy black-and-white films of Bigfoot, was that something moving through the trees? I kept watching, waiting. I could go back, but that would mean returning to the darkness. I went forward instead. Reaching the top, I paused under a huge oak and viewed the canyon before me. Immediately below was my yard. The corner of my screened porch was visible at the end of the near wall. Curiously, I neither saw nor heard dogs. From here I could see where my rusting wire fence with its rotting posts might be viewed by the dogs as more of a friendly suggestion than an actual physical boundary, like the basketball court lines painted on an asphalt playground. Still, shouldn't my dogs be down there sounding an alarm with me up here peering into our yard?

Maybe they were asleep on my flowered patio cushions. Really, where were those dogs?

Ernie and Alice's roof and part of Bryce's place were visible. Turning to the right, I could see all the way down the canyon road almost as far as the bridge, and at least parts of most of the homes in that direction. No wonder I had that sense of being watched. What a panorama these kids had!

A tiny bit of broken bark and two dry leaves floated down from the limbs above. A sound, no maybe just the feeling again of someone watching, someone breathing nearby. A small fluttery thing tickled down the back of my neck. A spider? I twitched, twisted, and grabbed my neck. Time to get out of there. Should I go forward, or return the way I had come? Again, going back meant returning to the darkness under the dense tree cover. The trail ahead ran along the ridge top, at least for a short distance. Anyway, I wanted to know where this trail led. I opted for forward.

The dirt pathway passed through dry grasses, much trampled at this time of year, and under a few scraggly blue oaks on the east side of the ridge. Then it topped the ridge and took off down the west slope underneath the darkness of thick live oaks. The trail was slick with shiny fallen leaves. Hoping this was a temporary turn, I plunged ahead.

Without warning, I was flying, then landed headfirst in a steep rocky depression to the side of the trail. A shower of leaves and broken branches fell around me. Tree bark, twigs, leaves and rocks tore at my face and hands as I slid. There was a ringing sound in my head, and maybe blackness. Then silence. The clanging in my head faded, but I lay still; moving seemed like a bad idea.

CHAPTER SEVEN

After some indeterminate period of fogginess, I became conscious of approaching footfalls. I tried to see what was coming, but dirt sifted onto my face and scalp, making my head itch. Something small and creepy slipped inside my collar and down my front. I chanced a weak call for help before the dirt filtered into my mouth, and, involuntarily, I spit. Yuck! Bad move.

"Oh my god, Miz Estela is that you?" It was Randy. Urgent whispering above and behind me, so someone else was there too. I couldn't imagine why they were whispering. Did they think I wouldn't be able to see them if I couldn't hear them? Randy stepped carefully down beside me, turned me gently and fumbled with my arms, trying to help me sit up. All my weight was downhill and there was nothing for me to grab ahold of to pull myself upright. He ended up getting under my shoulders and pushing from there. More dirt and crud shifted under the waistband of my jeans when I sat up. For sure I'd have to shower again when I got out of this mess.

Blood came away when I put my fingers to my cheek. While I was checking that out, tennis shoes scuffled in the dirt nearby and my second companion was gone, his pounding feet heading fast into the distance. I never saw who it was. I looked up at Randy, thinking about the fire and the death the night before. Was I in danger here?

About then I heard a voice off in the distance, moving closer. Must have been what scared the other guy off.

"Yoo-hoo! Yoo-hoo, Estela! Where are you, Estel..l..la? Yoo-hoo?" Betsy Carper. I never imagined I would be glad to hear her voice, and she was definitely coming this way.

"Oh, my! Oh, my! Oh, my! Estela what are you doing down there?" she exclaimed as she arrived on the scene. Her eyes widened, taking in Randy as well. "Well, Estela, this is a fine mess you're in."

It took all three of us, Betsy pulling, Randy pushing, and me scrambling on the slippery leaves, to get me up onto the trail. Stumbling, I reached up and discovered a tender knot rising on the back of my skull.

"Be careful!" Randy said, as we all regained our footing. He pointed to a wire strung across the trail, almost invisible. "This trail's booby trapped here. You gotta watch out."

If possible, Betsy's eyes grew wider still. "Oh, my! Booby trapped! Why, Randy, why is there a booby trap here?"

Randy cut me a quick look then rubbed his hand over his mouth. Body language for a reluctance to say something. "Just be careful," he muttered.

"I tripped on that wire?" I asked. "What the hell?" I rubbed my head again. Betsy looked with concern at the cut on my cheek. She dug out a tissue and handed it to me. I appreciated the gesture, but that tissue looked none too clean. I dusted my hands off and slipped the tissue into a pocket.

"I saw your car down there at Will's," she started, "and I knew you were up to something. I have a sense about these things. I looked around but I didn't see you anywhere. Then I heard a siren or something up here. Frightened me so, I almost went back to get Dick. Anyway, I found that place under the trees and the trail, so I came up this way. Then I heard someone crashing through the bushes. Very scary. Anyway, I couldn't imagine what you'd gotten up to out here, so I kept on and there you were, lying head-first in a ditch. It's a good thing I came along when I did, isn't it? What would you have done if I hadn't come along? Whatever are you doing up here anyway? You should sit down for a while."

Betsy knew a captive audience when she saw one. She looked around for a comfy place to park herself. She had all the time in the world. It was only my good fortune that she found nothing to sit on except dirt.

Sighing, Betsy settled in for a good long monologue on her feet. She began to regale Randy and me with her deductions about the recent goings-on in Arroyo Loco. Suffice to say, Betsy herself figured prominently in her story, both in the motives and as a target of the perpetrators.

Randy was shuffling impatiently. I interrupted Betsy to suggest that we get started in the direction of home. I pointed out that it was late afternoon and would soon be genuinely dark. I'm not going to say that fear was audible in my voice, but it was getting late and I was in increasing danger of missing a major meal.

"Oh, nonsense!" Betsy insisted. "I've already sent for Dick with my mind's eye. I have strong psychic powers, you know. Much stronger than anyone I know. I'm sure he'll be along shortly."

She mistook my look of horror for one of admiration and continued proudly, breaking into a happy smile. "Yes, do you know I am a witch? I joined the Wiccans many years ago, and I am a practicing witch." It might have been a bit of debris in her eye, but I think she winked at me. What the heck did that mean? Then a cloud passed across her happy expression and her shoulders slumped a little. "Of course," she went on, "most of those women who call themselves witches are nothing but attention-seeking cat lovers. They have no powers at all."

I stood in dumbfounded silence. Betsy must have sensed I had reached the end of my patience, as she began to sputter.

"Dick should be here any minute. We shouldn't try to walk on this trail by ourselves. He'll help us get back. I sent him a strong message. If he's not here in five minutes..." She took a couple of steps, peering up that way. I knew it was too dark to see anything at all. "I think I see him coming now," she said, gazing up to the top of the ridge.

Not having any luck with getting Betsy to move, I eased around her and started walking slowly along the trail, watching carefully for more wires.

"Randy, how many more of those booby traps are there out here?" I asked. His answer was to pull around to walk in front of us, shuffling carefully and repeating muttered apologies. He stopped every once in a while to point out places where small pits had been covered with twigs and leaves, and one other wire stretched across another turn on the trail. It was a miracle I had made it as far as I had without falling.

"Oh, shit, I'm so sorry this happened to you, Miz Estela...I'm gonna kill those stupid nacos. My bad, my bad. I told those guys to keep an eye out. I didn't say nothin' about booby trapping this trail. Man, I'm so sorry, Miz Estela!"

"Anywhoo," Betsy started again. "You know, I sent for Dick, Randy, but you must have gotten my message first. I do think you and I must have a strong psychic connection, Randy. I wonder whatever has happened to Dick. Well, no matter, we're so glad you're here to save us!"

I dug my flashlight out and cranked it as we walked, urging Betsy to keep walking. She grabbed my wrist, pointing the flashlight at her own feet. A few minutes later Randy pulled up, and we emerged into the clearing behind Will's house where the sky was lighter. Have I mentioned my neurotic fear of the dark? It wasn't until we made it back that I realized my beloved Giants baseball cap had gone missing in the fray. Damn! Well, I wasn't going looking for it, that's for sure.

Betsy stopped short, still chattering. Randy was cutting me urgent looks, and I wanted some answers. Although, by that point I really only wanted to get away from there.

"I wanna 'splain," he started, but was interrupted by Betsy. He tried again, and she over-talked him once more. Then he started shooting looks the other direction and tipping his head. Clearly, he wanted to say something, but not in front of Betsy. I wasn't sure what to do. Betsy's not that easy to shake.

She stopped chattering for a moment, and in the sudden silence we all heard it. A mournful plaintive call coming from downhill. I'll be the first to admit that I was very hungry, and that may have colored my hearing, but I could have sworn the voice was calling, "Custard! Custard!" Sounded like Helen.

I wanted to get home, shower, and eat. Or maybe eat and then shower. Sighing, I set off again in the direction of the voice, looking around for my companions. Randy was gone already, vanishing in utter silence. Guess they don't call those things sneakers for nothing. Betsy's face was pinched in a sour look. Yes, that was Helen's voice calling. Betsy turned and, without another word, headed off toward the road below.

Before I went too much farther, the call came again, this time very clearly. "Custard! Mocha! Here kitty, kitty. Please come home." Oh, cripes, her cats were lost. All set to tiptoe up the trail and go quietly home, I heard a familiar soft woof nearby. Then Helen appeared on the trail below me.

"Oh, Estela!" she wailed. "Someone cut a big hole in my cat cage, and Custard and Mocha are gone! Someone stole my precious, precious kitties!"

It seemed unlikely anyone would want two of Helen's cats enough to steal them. Sighing, I suggested we go look at the cage and search around there again. A roughly cat-sized hole had been cut in the heavy wire cage. Rather than being stolen, it looked like the cats could have simply walked on their own little paws through the hole to freedom.

Another familiar woof aroused my suspicions. Peering beyond a few trunks, I spotted my Scout's black and white body in a polite down at the base of one of the taller gray pines. He was pointing upward with his nose, and, sure enough, about fifteen feet up was a large, cream-colored, and very angry looking cat.

"Oh, my god!" Helen screamed. She crashed through the underbrush toward Scout, her shrill cry trailing behind. "He's going to kill her! He's killing her!"

There didn't seem to be any sense in pointing out that Scout was sitting quietly beside the tree, not trying to kill the cat. He was keeping her safely treed so she could not wander any farther. Also, he had signaled to the humans with his gentlest woof so they could come and find the vicious-looking but inexplicably adored feline. He gave Helen a bewildered look as she rushed toward him. Cat people are never going to understand dogs. When Helen started looking frantically around like she was searching for a weapon, I called Scout to my side and gave him a good hug and a ruffle. My border collies are trained to keep their distance from cats. Even the mildest looking kitten can rip a dog's face off in a nanosecond. Scout had done a good job of rounding up the cat and keeping it safely treed, and he deserved a kind word.

As if to prove my point, the minute Scout came to my side the cat braced its back feet against the tree and took a flying leap in the other direction, disappearing instantly into the chaparral. Scout easily could have rounded her up again and sent her up another tree for future safe retrieval, but clearly our assistance was not wanted here. With a relieved wave, I called to Helen that I would send help. She was last seen diving head first into the bushes under which the cat had vanished.

Scout and I were almost to the car when we were arrested by a pointed clearing of the throat to the side of the trail. We looked up, and there was Delia, perched uncomfortably on top of a particularly prickly looking hunk of granite, a large, ugly rifle across her lap. She was still wearing her bright-red Lycra and matching red band, not camo, so apparently this was not a secret mission. Guess I wasn't going to get that long, hot shower any time soon. Delia looked at me, down the canyon, then back at me.

"I'm keepin' an eye on Wally's house," she finally offered as explanation. "He ain't comin out, but he's got his car turned round pointin' out, and he's gonna make a run for it any minute now." She slowly raised the rifle to her eye and took a bead down canyon, I assumed on Wally's car which I couldn't see from my vantage point. "And I'm gonna get him when he do. Pow. Blow his brains out. Sayonara sucker."

"You've been watching too many Clint Eastwood movies, Delia. You know, you'll end up on Cell Block Nine if you do anything like that."

"You know what that damn sheriff's deputy told me?" Delia asked quietly, her rifle still pointed calmly at Wally's car. "He said Graciela and Sofia have to file charges before he can make a case against Wally." She lowered the rifle and looked at me. "Ain't that somethin'? We all know what he's doing, but we have to wait until he hurts our kids before the law will do anything."

I wasn't sure about that. What do I know? I could see where Delia would be frustrated. "Well," I said, "maybe Graciela will file charges, now that she has evidence."

"Nah. She's one a those niccy-nice ladies. She'll wish it would all go away. Me, I'm gonna blow it away. Soon's it shows its ugly rat face." She looked down canyon again.

"Say, Delia," I suddenly remembered. "You guys were gone last night during the fire, right?"

She looked at me cautiously. "Yeah," she said slowly, trying to figure where I was going with this question. Delia scares me. She's liable to go off at any time without warning, and I hate it when people yell at me, especially when they're holding a long, ugly looking, loaded rifle. I looked away like this was no big deal, and really, probably it wasn't.

"Well, do you know why there would have been a car parked in your driveway at about eight thirty last night?"

"A car in my driveway? What kinda car? Whose car?"

"It was a light-colored sedan, kind of a small car. I only saw it as it was backing out of the driveway, so I don't know how long it was there, or who was driving it."

Glancing at her own house behind her, she answered. "Nope. We left maybe six. It was still light. Me and Chamise and DeVon, we went to my sister's in Ojai. My niece is gettin' married next Sunday, so we had a thousand things to do. We didn't get home until this mornin', round ten." Something nagged at me when she said that, but I couldn't quite get what. She continued talking, looking at the bushes around her rock perch. "I'll tell you what did happen. I did almost run down Will when I was backing out."

"Oh?" I inquired, encouragingly.

"Didn't hit him, you understand? He only...it's only that he came to show me his spiders. We got into it that afternoon because he wanted to spray poison round my house. He said I had black widow spiders, and well, maybe I do, but I don't want that crazy old bastard spraying god knows what around my house!"

She was starting to rev up, so I replied calmly. "Hmm."

"Anyways, we got into a big screaming thing, you know how he is. He said I wouldn't know a black widow if it bit me, which is the truth, but I still don't want him spraying. Then he went away and came back a while later with this jar with one of those things in it and showed us, both Chamise and me. They are mean-lookin' bugs, with that big, shiny belly and red hourglass thing painted underneath."

"So, that's when you almost ran him down?"

"No. Well, yes, sort of. I mean, we were gettin' ready to leave. I went in the house and got my keys, gathered up stuff and whatnot, got in the car, and, well," she paused. "I let DeVon drive on account of him gettin' his license soon, and he backed up a little fast. Seemed like Will woulda been long gone, but I guess he don't move that fast anymore."

I furrowed my brow. Although she was only glancing at me occasionally while telling this story, I wanted to be ready with my concerned-psychotherapist look, so she would feel comfortable telling the whole story and wouldn't leave out any potentially significant details.

"Will was right there at the end of the drive and when DeVon came at him with the back end of that big ole SUV, and well, Will sort of tripped and fell into the ditch. He was okay. I mean, he wasn't knocked out or anything cause he was flailing around down there. He shook his fist at me good when we backed past him. I woulda stopped to help, but he was righteously mad. He'd probably have taken a swing at me. He was climbing out as we drove off, so I know he was okay. It's only, he was mad."

We both took a few long breaths. "Maybe he hit his head and passed out later," I speculated. Delia began to draw herself up, turned her gaze to mine and reddened. Hastily I added, "But I'm sure he was fine. It sounds like he was fine. Why don't you get down off that uncomfortable rock and put that mean-looking thing away?" I said, referring to the rifle. "Somebody cut the wire on Helen's cat cage and a couple of them got out. She could really use help rounding them up. She didn't appreciate the services of a herding dog."

"Humph." Delia continued to glare at me. Then, grumbling, she started to climb down. She slipped toward the end and slid the rest of the way directly onto the arch of my right foot. I'm sure that was a complete accident. It still hurts, but in the interest of ending what had already been a long day, I didn't say a word. I hobbled off in the direction of my car, my cozy home, and a hot dinner.

As Scout and I cleared Will's garage, my car finally in sight, Lauren appeared, giving me quite a start. I'd had enough surprises for one day.

"Oops, sorry." She put her hand to her mouth. "Didn't mean to scare you."

"Were you watching me?" I asked, somewhat irritated.

Lauren smiled in her impish way. "Of course," she affirmed. "I saw you drive up and park. You walked to the place behind Will's. Then you went off down the trail, came up again, and went off that way," she pointed. "Then Betsy came tiptoeing along after you. Time passed, and I thought about going to look for you, but then you all came trooping back, and about that time Helen started to wail. I was afraid Delia was going to shoot her."

Dumbfounded, my mouth dropped open. What were we all doing here, putting on a little performance for Lauren? Apparently, she already knew all about the trail. Does she sit up there in her upstairs office and surveil all the goings-on at Arroyo Loco? Maybe editing technical journals is a cover story. Maybe her real job is to keep an eye on all of us. I must be getting punchy. Who would want to keep an eye on the minutiae of life in our hamlet? Finally, I stopped making like a goldfish, and closed my mouth. For her part, Lauren didn't seem to be the least bit self-conscious about watching all of our shenanigans.

"I came out," she continued, "to tell you that after some research on the computer, I've confirmed that Wally is registered on the sex offender's web site, www.meganslaw.ca.gov. It shows on that registry that Wally has spent time in prison for doing the same type of crime when they lived in Ventura. Twice. Two felony convictions. He served his last sentence at the nearby Men's Colony. That's probably why Tina moved here, to be close to him while he was locked up." Behind those thick lenses, Lauren cut an angry scowl in the direction of Wally's house. I felt empty. To think a pedophile was living that close and hurting children I knew, children who lived all around me. I was beginning to feel like I was channeling Delia's anger. That was scary.

"Thanks," I said. "Want to or not, we all need to know that. Let's get the word out. I can't wait until Monday, when the sheriff's people get back to work and their office can take this whole thing over. What a mess." Lauren nodded solemnly.

Taking a deep breath, I stepped back mentally, trying to get a feel for the bigger picture. We both strolled onto the road where we could see the burned out house. "Do you think this thing with Wally has anything to do with the fire and the guy dying? I mean, do you think there's a connection?" I asked.

"Sort of seems like..." Lauren trailed off.

"Yeah," I agreed. "It's like one of those too-big-to-be-a-coincidence things, huh?"

She nodded again. "So, what do you think happened?" It occurred to me that if Lauren had been watching me all afternoon, she might know more than she was letting on about other things or, at least, have some insights.

We wandered over and settled on her steps. After anointing her lantana bush, my dogs started romping in the small front yard. Hey, wait a second! I looked around and sure enough, both dogs were now with me. Honestly, why did I bother with a fence?

"Well," Lauren started, "Delia and Will had that big fight yesterday. Delia was so mad. Her car almost knocked him into that ditch when she was leaving."

Startled, I asked "She knocked him, or he fell?"

"She came pretty close. Any of us would have jumped or fallen, as fast as she was backing up and as close as she came."

I nodded, then wondered why Lauren hadn't mentioned that before. She went on. "He got out okay, but either he cut himself on that glass jar you found, or one of those spiders bit him because he was holding his arm."

The slam of Freda's screen door distracted our attention as she came toward us bearing, bless her heart, a plate of food. When she got close, I could see they were cookies.

She held the plate out. "Spitzbuben?"

"Excuse me?"

Freda chuckled. "They are Austrian jam cookies. Spitzbuben."

"Oh," I said, reaching for one. "Yummy." While I nibbled a couple more, Lauren went inside and reappeared a few minutes later with a large, cold can of organic juice, plastic cups, and a dampened paper towel, which she handed to me, gesturing at my cheek. Guess it didn't look so good.

"Sorry, " she said. "We only drink fair trade coffee and we're out." She paused. "Ah, the truth is, we have plenty but Valerie doesn't want to share."

After we settled into recyclable bamboo chairs, I caught Freda up on the conversation. "Lauren was telling me that Will fell down yesterday afternoon, in that ditch there in front of Delia's." I pointed. "Did you see that, Freda?"

"Who me? Oh no, I try not to look in that direction if I don't have to!" She lowered her voice to a whisper, and leaned close, "Crazy people!" The lines at the corners of her eyes crinkled and she smiled. "Here, have some more Spitzbuben. They're very small." She offered the plate again, and I helped myself to a couple more.

"So, Lauren, what time was it that Will fell?"

"Six o'clock on the dot. I know because I had to go down and start dinner. Valerie has a fit if I start five minutes late."

"I saw a car in Delia's driveway at about eight thirty," I chipped in. "Did you see that?"

Lauren dropped her chin into her hands and looked off into space. Her lenses reflected the dying light so that I couldn't see her eyes at all, and the expression on her face was hard to read. "Not really," she finally said. "We ate in the dining room, and after that we packed a few boxes of stuff out of the hutch. We were in the dining room for a couple of hours. I did see the car driving off at about eight thirty, but I didn't see it arrive, or who was in it. I thought it was somebody visiting the Jacksons, but I guess they weren't home."

"No," I agreed. "Delia says they were gone all night." That's when it hit me. When Helen and I passed Delia's house this morning, between ten and eleven o'clock, she came out in her bathrobe as though she hadn't yet gotten dressed for the day. According to her story, she and the kids arrived home at about that time. Something didn't fit there.

"Shoot," Lauren said. "I wish I'd seen who was in the car and knew where they were going." She paused, "I did see you and the dogs strolling by a few minutes after that."

"Thank goodness!" I exclaimed with genuine relief. Good to know there was a reliable eyewitness to verify my innocent whereabouts at the time the crime, or crimes, had been committed.

CHAPTER EIGHT

With wide eyes, Freda asked, "If you were looking out the window at eight thirty last night, did you see the fire?"

"Ah, no, Freda, I didn't see the fire. I was passing the window, not standing there looking out. It may have started already...I just didn't see it."

The three of us turned to look toward what was left of the house. From this angle, I had to lean way out to my right to see Will's front porch. If the fire had been burning in the back when Lauren looked out, she still couldn't have seen it from here.

There was a shuffle off to our left. We snapped in that direction and saw Helen dragging herself up the walk. Her face and arms were scratched, the long sleeve of her shirt was torn, and a piece of brush dangled in the blonde hair over her right ear. She clutched a crumpled, half-eaten bag of chips in one arm.

"Helen!" I exclaimed. "Did you catch the cats?"

"No," she moaned. "We got Custard, but Mocha is still out there." Her gaze shifted toward the darkening ridge line behind her house. "Delia sent DeVon over and Randy came along. They're out there looking. I fell and twisted my wrist. It's getting dark. I can't look anymore. I gave them the bag of kibble to shake." She looked down at Shiner and Scout, who were sitting obediently at her feet, hoping for a potato chip offering. "You know how they'll come running when they hear the kibble rattling in the bag? Too bad I can't send the electric can opener out there with the boys. Those cats really come running when they hear the can opener." We all nodded. Heck, I come running when I hear a can opener.

"I also gave them a cat carrier so they could set a trap. It's possible Mocha will come for food, but more likely I'll never see him again." She sighed. "At least Custard and Spumoni are safely at home."

I found myself hoping Spumoni stays in her house forever because I, personally, do not ever want to see a cat the color of Spumoni. My thoughts must have been broadcast on my face because Helen cut me a look.

"She's not really pink and green and brown, Stel," she assured me in a slightly nasty tone. "She's a calico. Three colors."

I nodded and tried not to look too relieved. I'm really going to have to work on better face control. After a few moments of respectful silence, I returned to the previous topic.

"Good. Well, we were talking about what we know about what happened, you know, with the fire and all. We know Will was alive as late as six o'clock last night. That's when he fell into the ditch. He got out and made it home. After that we don't know. It seems like he laid down in his bed and died for some reason we don't know about. Maybe he was bitten by a black widow spider. Maybe he had a heart attack. Maybe he hit his head when he fell. We do think he may have been bleeding from a cut on his arm..." I had an idea. "Lauren, was he holding his arm, like his arm was hurt, or was it his wrist, or what?"

"Ah, kind of his forearm. Like this," she demonstrated a hold on her forearm closer to her wrist.

"Hmm. So, what if he gashed his wrist open on the broken glass and bled to death? I don't think that sort of thing would still be visible, given what's left of him now," I paused. "Anyway, he walked home and then died in bed."

"Okay, but I don't remember there being any blood on the broken glass," Helen said. "It was clean."

"Yeah, that's true," I considered that. "And we didn't see any blood in the ditch or trailing along toward his porch." Everyone nodded in agreement. "Maybe we should cross that off the list. So, he just died?"

"That's kind of a stretch, Stel," Helen said. "The guy just laid down and died?"

"Yeah." Heck, I didn't know. "Remember, it might not be Will who died. It might have been Kenneth. He was sick apparently, really sick, so maybe he died and somebody put his body there."

Lauren looked puzzled. "Somebody drove up in a small sedan, unloaded Kenneth's body, carried it into the house, and thought no one would see them?" she asked, incredulous.

"Oh, that is a stretch," Freda nodded.

"Yeah," I agreed. "Not very likely, huh? Although the car did arrive without anyone seeing it, or anyone we know about anyway, and no one knows how long it was there. So anything's possible..." We all sat there thinking about the possibilities.

Lauren wrapped up our thoughts. "The body might have been someone else, but it makes the most sense if it was Will, however he ended up dead."

"Yeah, I agree. Remember, his car is sitting there in the garage. If Will is still alive and someone else died in his bed, why isn't he off somewhere driving his own car?"

"Maybe he faked his own death and planted someone else's body," Nina said from beside the lantana. Where did she come from and how long had she been standing there?

"That sounds like one of those classic mystery plots from Perry Mason," Helen chuckled. There was a murmuring of agreement. Faking his own death was an elegant explanation, but hatching a well-thought-out diabolic plan like that was not our Will.

Nina settled in on a step and reached for the plate of cookies on my lap. "What happened to you?" she asked. "You look like a wreck. There's a scrape on your cheek. Helen looks worse. What did I miss?"

I touched my face absently. There was definitely going to be a nasty bruise there. Taking a deep breath, I considered the potential consequences of relating the whole story of my afternoon adventures to all of them. I decided against that. Instead, I said I'd taken a nasty fall while hiking. They were all suitably horrified and sympathetic.

"You know, I've been thinking..." Helen said in a speculative tone. "Will did have that big fight with Delia, and Delia is a home health nurse. She has access to some powerful drugs. Is it possible she drugged Will, then set that house on fire?" Interesting idea. Delia did drive away long before the fire started, and no one saw her return. Then again, there was that sedan in her driveway while she was gone. We were stumped.

"Hmm," I continued to ponder the question. "So, you know, we may have to wait for the medical examiner to tell us who died in that fire, and exactly how they died. Unless someone confesses, we can't figure that out ourselves, but what about the fire? We should be able to reason out who had the means, motive, and opportunity to start that fire. What do we know?"

"Well, those people in the car started it, don't you think?"

"Ah, no," Lauren jumped in to explain. "Freda, they couldn't have because they left at eight thirty, and you called the fire in at about quarter after nine. A gasoline fire like that would be more like an explosion."

"Yeah," I agreed. "I strolled past the house at about quarter to nine, and I didn't see anything either. What it all boils down to is opportunity. We all had motive, some more likely than others. The means was the gasoline and a match..."

"Or a lit cigarette," Helen interjected.

"Yeah, or a lit cigarette. So, it's opportunity that's the key here. Who had the opportunity to carry a bright-red five-gallon can filled with gasoline to Will's sometime that evening, and set it on fire at about nine o'clock?"

"We all hate Wally," Nina said. "Can't we find someway to pin this on Wally?" That garnered cynical smiles of agreement all around.

"If Will or Janet had anything to do with those photographs, Wally had a better motive than anyone else to kill them and destroy their house," Helen said.

"I wish we could at least hang the fire on Wally," I agreed. "But he was in the roadhouse when the fire started. I saw him come out when the alarm went off."

"Well, how long had he been in there?" Helen asked.

"Good point," I said. "I could ask Ernie or Thomas. They were there too."

Nina said excitedly, "Yes! He lit the fire then scurried off like a little mouse before the alarm went off!" She made scurrying motions with her fingers heading off toward the roadhouse.

"Oh, but then you were walking down the road, Estela. Would you not have seen if Wally started the fire, then went scurrying down to the roadhouse?" Freda made the same scurrying motions with her fingers. Very amusing, but she made a good point. It's a fair distance from the rear of Will's house to the roadhouse. My dogs and I would have seen anyone running down along the road.

"Maybe there was a long fuse or some way to delay the start of the fire," I suggested. "Or maybe it started more like a little before nine, and it got a slow start." Everyone sat and thought that one through.

About then Amanita's dark green sedan rolled into view coming down canyon. She was staring intently at the Rosenblums' house as she passed and very nearly drove right into the same ditch into which Will had fallen. She corrected at the last minute, then noticed Lauren, Nina, Freda, Helen, and me sitting around Lauren's front porch. She gave no sign of recognition, but slowed to a crawl and stared out at us with a scowl, her small head barely clearing the windowsill. She peered at us as, doubtlessly hoping to catch us planting some forbidden non-drought-tolerant bush in Lauren's front yard. Nina turned and gave Amanita a little finger wave, but the rest of us watched as she rolled past. Nina really is one of those nicey-nice ladies, as Delia would put it.

After she had passed, Helen spoke up, "Okay, I've got it. Wally poured the gasoline, intending to burn those incriminating photographs and Will along with them. Then, for some reason, he didn't light the fire. Maybe he forgot the matches and went home to get some. Maybe he didn't have any and had to go all the way down to the roadhouse to get some. Then the fire started some other way while Wally was in the roadhouse."

"You're crazy, Helen," Nina said flatly. "How does a fire start—even when there's gasoline—how does it start by itself?"

"Hmm," I speculated. "Maybe someone did toss a cigarette butt back there."

Looking at the floor, Lauren said, "One of the kids, you mean." That was a sad thought.

Freda had some other ideas. "Oh, I see. Will killed himself with a self-inflicted spider bite, and put his own body in the bed. Then someone came and put the ring on his finger..."

A couple of us cried out simultaneously, "The person in the sedan!"

"Yes," Freda continued, "the person in the sedan. Then Wally poured the gasoline and went away. Then a teenager threw the cigarette butt and, kaboom!" Her hands flew up and out, miming an explosion. "You know, like Agatha Christie and the murder on the Orient Express! All different people making the murder!"

Wow, yeah! We were impressed with our collectively brilliant powers of deduction.

"Each one is guilty of some part of the crime, but no one is guilty of all of it," she concluded.

The front door creaked open slightly and Valerie poked her head out. Her narrowed eyes landed on each of us briefly. "Honey, are we having juice and cookies for dinner? It's almost six." She glared at Lauren, who jumped up and quickly gathered the juice can and plastic cups. Helen and I shot each other suspicious glances, still wondering about Valerie's possible guilt.

"Yeah, we're only going around in circles here anyway," I said. "I've got to get these guys home. See you ladies later." The dogs and I trotted off as everyone else scattered too, waving as they went.

Once safely onto my screened porch, I peeled each shoe off with the toe of the other foot. Scooping kibble into the dog dishes, I carried them into the kitchen and put them down where the contents were instantly vacuumed up by two hungry beasts. I returned my outerwear carefully to the closet, noting a new tear in my prized insect-repellant shirt. That would require mending, since it is my intention to be buried in that shirt. I snapped the deadbolt closed, something I rarely do. My slippers were waiting for me in front of the recliner. I located the remote control, unhooked my bra with one hand, and drew it off under my shirt. Ah! I didn't feel like walking all the way down the hall to put it away, so gave it a fling in that general direction. I don't know if this is common knowledge, but brassieres are not all that aerodynamic. Mine landed in a twisted pile about six feet away in the middle of the hall.

Food next, and I considered my options. Unlike some of the better-known sleuths, I did not have ready access to a McDonald's drive thru for a Big Mac with cheese and large fries. I had to settle for a couple of slices of two-day-old leftover Mama O'Brien's pizza, nuked and served ala carte. At least it was a double-mushroom-and-olive pizza and not one of those anemic thin-crusted artichoke-heart-and-slivers-of-pepper things. Popping the top on a can of Bud Light to round out the menu, I settled deeply into the fuzzy, brown recliner, pizza and beer at the ready on the end table.

As my head hit the backrest, I remembered about Randy trying to get my attention earlier. What was it he wanted to tell me? How could I track him down to ask? Randy seemed to appear and disappear around here, without ever being in any one place too long. His mother Catherine often complained that he only came home weekday mornings to shower and collect his lunch money, then was gone again. I'd have to wait until he chose to reappear before I could find out what he wanted to say.

I was reaching for the first slice of pizza when, of course, the telephone rang. Oh, great. This was exactly the very last thing I needed. And to make it worse, the display said, "Private Caller." Who are these people who expect me to answer my phone when I don't know who is interrupting my evening? I thrashed around in the recliner, but couldn't quite reach the phone without getting out of the chair entirely. Oh, the heck with it, I decided. I'll let the machine get Mr. Private Caller. That's when Shiner poked the handset with his snout, knocking it onto the floor.

"Hello? Hello?" A tiny female voice called into the dust under my end table. "Hello?"

Shiner looked at me expectantly, then at the phone. He barked. Something to keep in mind should a life of crime ever appeal: border collies may not look vicious, but they know how to answer a telephone. And for his next trick, I'm going to teach him to dial 911.

"Hello?" came again from the voice of Ms. Private Caller.

I struggled out of the chair, hobbled around, and retrieved the handset from amid the dust bunnies. Wiping it off, I grunted irritably into the device. Of all people, it was Tina, Wally's wife.

Without further preamble, she asked, "Why is there a blue plastic bucket in your driveway?"

Struck dumb. I pulled the phone away from my ear and looked at it, as though it would explain itself. Tina was muttering, apparently to someone in the room with her. "I know, I know," she whispered. Sounded like Wally was close behind her, telling her to ask again, which she did.

"Why do you have a blue bucket in your driveway?" she demanded more insistently.

Wally has Tina completely intimidated, and if he was standing right behind her forcing her to make this call, I didn't want to make life any harder than it already was for her. But really, what was the appropriate response here?

"Uh, I used it to wash something?" I tried tentatively.

"Oh. You used it to wash something," she repeated carefully, relaying the information to her audience.

"Yeah, I used it to wash my car. I guess I forgot to put it away."

"Oh, you forgot to put it away," she relayed again.

"Yeah."

"Oh. Okay, all right." For a moment, it seemed she was going to stop there, but then she went on. "It's only that where we used to live..." She started over, "In Ventura where we used to live, the drug dealers would put out something like that to signal when they were open for business. We just wondered...umph!" Her air was expelled suddenly, like someone had punched her. "I just wondered," she corrected, "if it was something like that."

"Uh, no, nothing like that." I suppose I could have elaborated, but really, what the hell was this about anyway? Was she accusing me of being a drug dealer?

There was more urgent muffled conversation on the other end of the line and then Tina was back. "Uh, there wasn't gasoline in the bucket was there?"

"No." Still wondering where this was going.

"Cause we...I...thought maybe there was gasoline in your bucket. I walked by earlier today and it smelled like gasoline."

"No, there was water in it." What the heck?

More mumbling from Tina. If I had to guess I'd say she was shuffling through pages of a script on her end of the conversation.

She started again. "You know, Estela, Wally didn't have anything to do with that fire at Will's, or with killing him. You know that, right?"

Hmm, interesting. It didn't seem like a good idea to give a direct answer to that question, so I tried a different tack.

"It might not have been Will who died, Tina. Some people think it was Kenneth, Janet's brother."

"Oh," she replied with relief. "Well, Wally especially didn't kill Kenneth!" A pause, "And you know, spilling gasoline isn't a crime, you know... umph!" again. "Uh, never mind."

This whole conversation was strange. It crossed my mind that maybe I should try to milk it for more information. "I beg your pardon?"

"Uh, nothing. It's just, spilling gasoline isn't a crime." She gave a desperate sounding sigh. Abruptly, the phone clicked a disconnect.

Fine. Now my pizza was cold and taking on the consistency of water-logged cardboard. Why is it that food reheated in the microwave cools off so much faster than food heated in the oven? Isn't hot, hot? I returned the pizza to the microwave again, knowing that would give it the consistency of rubberized wet cardboard. While waiting, I looked out through the screened porch. In the dim glow of the porch bulb, I could see the faint outline of the bucket. Out of pure curiosity, I stepped outside, Scout following close behind me. Maybe it was my imagination, but he seemed more reluctant than usual to let me out of his sight. I leaned down and sniffed the bucket. Yup. Someone had definitely put a little gasoline into that blue plastic bucket. I looked around. Ernie and Alice can see my driveway when they are sitting on their front porch, and they do often sit out there. So maybe they saw someone in my driveway earlier today. On the other hand, it was October, so probably they weren't doing a lot of porch-sitting. Other than Ernie and Alice, only Amanita and the people driving to the house under construction at the top of the canyon might have seen something.

My initial reaction was to rush the bucket inside and wash it thoroughly, but then I realized, that would only make me look guilty. According to those shows on television, cops have ways of finding minute traces of things like gasoline in the drain of a laundry sink. I decided to leave the contents alone, although I did move the bucket up closer to the house. Better to be thought a slob, or worse, a drug dealer open for business, than to panic and incriminate myself further in this murder. After all, whoever put the gasoline in there didn't know I had the best alibi going. Deputy Muñoz had seen me bring it out and pour water onto his tire. He knew there was no gasoline in it this morning.

Back inside, I wandered toward my home office for my laptop, skirting the brassiere. If leaving a plastic bucket in my driveway meant I was a drug dealer open for business, what would Wally and Tina think the bra in a heap on the hall floor signaled? I picked it up and put it away. As long as I was passing through the bedroom, I changed my dirty jeans for some cozy fleece sweats and pulled on my favorite well-worn hoodie. The hoodie would give me instant bed head, but what the heck. I wasn't going out again tonight.

Finally resettled with pizza and beer, I flipped open the laptop and logged on, giving the dial-up connection plenty of time to load my email. I hadn't checked since last Thursday and should see what my cousin, Diego, was up to, or if he needed anything. He usually did, and it usually started with the initial $. Diego is the only child of my favorite cousin. I think that makes him a cousin once or twice removed, but I'm not sure about that. He is finishing up his junior year at the university and, like most students today, is swamped in education debt. We share the experience of being an only child enmeshed in a sprawling clan of cousins, and since I have no children of my own, we've sort of adopted one another.

My heart sank as new messages slowly scrolled down the page. The very first one was from Bryce to the entire community and its subject line yelled, all in caps:

EMERGENCY HOA MEETING
I opened it and read the rest.

Saturday, tonight, there will be a Mandatory Emergency Meeting of the Arroyo Loco Home Owner Association. All residents are required to attend. Some of you are accused of serious wrongdoing in the fire that destroyed the home of Wilhelm and Janet Rosenblum and the death of an unidentified person or persons in that home. The meeting begins promptly at 7:00 p.m.!!!

My gaze slid to the current time. 6:38 p.m. Great. Twenty minutes to put my clothes on again, make myself presentable, and get there. Hell, it would take twenty minutes just to chew this pizza.

I clicked reply and wrote an "urgent" email to Nina to ask if she was going, adding the enticement that I had some juicy gossip to share. Nina leaves her computer on all the time and listens for incoming messages, so I was sure she'd get my message in a minute or two. As an example of the quality of my material, I included the tidbit about Betsy being a witch. "We might all refer to Amanita as a witch, but Betsy told me she really is one," I said. In the nanosecond after my finger hit the "send" button my brain registered the "reply to all" in the address line, but it was too late. The entire community would receive my message and there was nothing I could do about it now.

I briefly considered fleeing as far from Arroyo Loco as I could get on half a tank of gas, and then staying there forever. Not feasible. Instead, I struggled up again and, still chewing my pizza, went off to put my clothes back on. There wasn't time to brush my teeth, so I swished a swallow of beer and let it go at that. I was pulling on my much-less-favored Oakland A's baseball cap when the cheery ding of my computer receiving email sounded. It dinged again before I could get there, and then again, twice in a row. By the time I'd dragged it onto my lap, there were five answers to my "reply to all" gaffe. Apparently, Nina isn't the only one who leaves her email open all the time. And some of those subject lines didn't look at all friendly or cheery. I only opened Nina's message, for which the subject line read simply, "oops."

Her message said Bryce had jumped the gun in sending his announcement, and the emergency meeting would be held tomorrow, Sunday morning, at 10:00 a.m. She added that since we were not being held prisoner in Arroyo Loco, the meeting was not truly mandatory, but she "wouldn't miss it for the world."

My computer dinged twice more. I turned it off in mid-ding. After giving the dogs their teeth-cleaning biscuits, we all headed for bed and a good book. I did stop to really brush my own teeth on the way.

Going to bed and going to sleep are not the same thing. I read for quite a long time. Then for a while, I stared at the ceiling thinking about those booby traps on the trail that afternoon and wondering what Randy was up to out there. As I was considering rolling over and getting serious about this falling asleep thing, both dogs startled and lifted their heads. Dogs have a way of acting like they can see through walls. Maybe with that well-developed sense of smell and their acute hearing, they really can sense what we cannot see. Scout and Shiner alerted and stared at the wall like they had X-ray vision. Part of me figured they were only playing, getting a kick out of scaring me. The other part of me was freaking out. Quickly, I got up and made the rounds again, double-checking that doors were locked, windows secured, and that there were no gaps in the drapes. The part I hate is going up to a blackened window, being exposed to anyone out there, and knowing that one day a pasty face and staring eyeballs are going to be peering in at me from out of the night. And why is that split second after I've flipped the deadbolt scarier than the second before? I've always felt like I got that bolt locked the instant before some horrible creature pushed the door open and grabbed me. After my experience that afternoon, I was still on edge.

I climbed back in bed, but all that rushing around checking doors and windows had frightened me to the point where sleep was not going to be mine any time soon. Getting up again, I turned on lights in other parts of the house, and went back to bed. A few minutes later the dogs alerted again, and this time I definitely heard something creeping around outside. Maybe it was only a branch breaking in the breeze. Or the arsonist pouring gasoline around my house. We would all die in a fiery blaze, locked up securely in our cozy little home.

Oh, cripes, I was never going to fall asleep this way. It wasn't even ten o'clock, so picking up the bedside phone, I dialed Helen's number. We could talk about her missing cat or something.

After a brief conversation, I admitted my call was really about me being scared. "Maybe we should get together and have a slumber party or something?" I suggested. "Nobody would bother us if we were all together."

"Well, that sounds like a good idea, but I'm not leaving my cats alone. You would all have to come here."

"Hmm. Except I'm not leaving my dogs alone, and it's hard to see how the dogs and cats would mix." I was thinking about how much I didn't want my dogs' faces to get ripped off, and I'm sure Helen was picturing her cats getting torn to pieces. As if!

"We can't go to Nina's," she said. "It's way too small."

"And Lauren's is big enough, but then there's Valerie," I said. "And can you imagine all of us, and the cats and the dogs in Freda's glass and china museum! It would be pure chaos!" We both had a good laugh over that one. "Yeah, I guess we're all staying home tonight," I concluded. "Let's keep an eye out and watch over each other."

"Okay, I guess you're right," she agreed, and we ended our conversation.

After laughing with Helen, I did feel better. It was hard to see how I was going to keep an eye out with all of my window shades drawn, but the conversation and laughter had calmed me down some. At least the dogs were here with me. I invited Shiner onto the bed, where, after circling the requisite three times, he curled up with his warm back pressed against my own. If something really bad went down, he would alert me. With those comforting thoughts, I did eventually drift off to a fitful sleep. As it turned out, there wasn't a whole lot of sleeping going on anywhere in Arroyo Loco that night.

CHAPTER NINE

I did not leap out of bed and go on a nice long run Sunday morning, like some of those more popular detectives. I was finishing a second cup of Costa Rican Fair Exchange organic coffee, sitting peacefully in the morning sun on my screened porch with my dogs and a good book when the time for the emergency HOA meeting rolled around. I considered what to do about the dogs. Leaving them outside alone wasn't an option. They'd only get out and come after me anyway. Ordinarily, they could be left inside, but not with an arsonist loose in the neighborhood. I could take the Subaru and they could stay there during the meeting, but that didn't sound safe either. The only way that felt safe was to keep them with me, and rules about dogs in the roadhouse would have to be damned. Grabbing clean old towels to keep them off the cold wood roadhouse floor, I leashed them, and locked the door, something that I hadn't done in a long time. This was hellish, living in a place where neighbors couldn't be trusted not to murder neighbors in bed and torch their houses.

As we approached, I could see Deputy Muñoz's big white SUV pulled directly in front, exactly where parking was not allowed. Alice sat inside, animatedly chatting with him, her fluffy white head bobbing up and down as she talked. Was Alice arrested? Arroyo Loco gets more loco by the minute.

The dogs and I filed quietly past. I was trying not to stare, but it looked like Alice had gotten to a serious part, and the deputy was writing stuff down in his notebook. She sure had a lot to say.

The chairs were already circled in the meeting room. The faint fragrance of woodsmoke from roadhouse days was still perceptible this cold morning, as was the faintest scent of barbecuing ribs and slightly spoiled coleslaw. Bryce was setting up the stand for the large pad of newsprint where proceedings are recorded. We used to have someone take minutes for the meetings, but there were always huge arguments later about what had been discussed and decided, so we gave up that. Now the minutes are recorded on the newsprint as we go along. This does not eliminate arguments; it only shifts them from a week after the meeting to during the meeting, when hurt feelings are still fresh and misunderstandings and confusions still hot. The delays can be endless. I don't know who's in charge of keeping track of all those large pads of newsprint either. I'm only glad it's not me.

Trying to stay out of the spotlight, I slid into the chair next to Sunshine. She coughed uncomfortably and did not acknowledge my arrival, but she also didn't get up and move. I put the dogs' towels down close behind my chair. Raymond was a couple of seats to the left of Sunshine. He may be the president of our group, but he only talks at meetings if he genuinely has something to say, and Sunshine is usually fairly quiet too, so I was hoping this would be the less noticed side of the circle.

Shiner turned around three times and settled behind me on his towel. Scout sat in front, leaning against my knee. A few chairs to my right, Nina was making space for

Margaret's wheelchair while Thomas waited to wheel his mother's chair into place. Nina didn't make eye contact with me, and I couldn't really fault her for that. Who doesn't check the reply line when sending an email?

Tina and Wally sat across the circle, empty chairs on either side. Dull black hair hid her eyes. She huddled there in a cowl-necked, olive-green, oversized sweater, picking nervously at pills and loose threads. When she saw me looking, she pulled her feet closer and scrunched her head down, like a giant startled turtle. Wally just stared. His feet were crossed primly at his ankles, an enigmatic expression on his face, like some eerie mannequin. Was that a smirk? What was he thinking? Impossible to tell. The only movement was one foot tapping, tapping, tapping. Mesmerizing. On the chair next to Tina sat a small tape recorder.

Amanita was arranging sage and other "sacred" plants on a small table. She often made an "offering to the spirits" on special occasions. She wasn't usually specific about which spirits. She turned and stared, not at me, but at my dogs. Resolutely, she started toward the three of us, a nasty remark on the tip of her tongue, I'm sure. Then she glanced at the glower on my face, and her eyes flashed fear. Scout turned slowly to look at her and lifted one side of his upper lip. With Amanita, the only genuinely effective defense is an assertive and preemptive offense. Deepening my glare, I growled, "Back off, Amanita. They're staying." She stopped, teared up, and veered toward Bryce. They put their heads together whispering, while she whimpered and pointed at me.

"Psst! Psssst!" I turned. Helen gestured urgently at me from the darkened rear corner. Graciela and Sofia stood there with her. Trying not to disturb Scout, who was turning circles on his towel, getting ready to sleep, I eased over there, smile-nodding at Sofia, who looked mortified to be there with her mother.

Having had considerable experience counseling troubled young people at the university, I wondered what Sofia would say if we could find a time and place to talk. The clients who come to me in my office are there because they want to talk. Sofia did not look like she wanted to talk to anyone. I could only imagine how confused and horrified she must have felt.

Helen was hissing in that annoying way again. I flashed her an irritated glance. Shifting my attention to Graciela, my eyes turned to pools of liquid sympathy as I switched on my concerned-psychotherapist expression.

Graciela is pretty and always perky. She is the original eternal optimist, and never has a negative thought. She was having none of my sympathy. Then again, she did have Sofia more or less chained to her side. If it was me, I would also have had Wally's scalp hanging off my belt, but we've already established that I might not be the most levelheaded person in Graciela's situation.

"Listen. Listen to this, Stel," Helen whispered. "Graciela saw the people in the sedan! It was Janet! And her brother Kenneth!" I turned with surprise to Graciela.

"Yes," she nodded. "They stopped by the office about eight thirty last night. I was out in front because I forgot to bring in my real estate sign again. They were leaving the mailboxes, then they pulled across and stopped here."

"Did Janet say anything? What did she say?" Helen asked.

I interrupted, "This was a light-colored sedan, and it came from somewhere up the canyon road?"

Graciela nodded, "Yes, yes. They were here when I first saw them. They pulled over and stopped beside me."

"So what did Janet say?" I asked.

"She got out of the car, but the man with her didn't. She introduced him as her brother, Kenneth, but I didn't get a good look at him. He was driving. It was most definitely not Will. He looked fine to me. Anyway, Janet said hello, asked how we were, and asked for a business card. She said she might need some help and asked for the card. Then they drove off up the highway," she waved, indicating the inland direction.

"Hmm," I said. "Interesting. She might need some help as in, she might need help selling her house?"

"I don't know. Maybe," Graciela smiled, prospects of sales commissions dancing in her eyes. "She was very sweet, but that's all she said."

"Did she seem confused, or excited, or anything?" Helen inquired, shooting me a knowing glance.

"No, no, not really. Not in a hurry. You know, kind of sad, but smiling. She's always like that. Only asked for the card, thanked me, and they drove away."

"Did she tell you how to get in touch with her?" I asked. "Do you have a phone number for her, or any way to contact her?"

Graciela shook her head. "No, the deputy already asked me that. Janet said she'd call me. Ordinarily, I would get at least a phone number for a potential client, but she said no, that she would call me."

Helen and I nodded solemnly. This was an interesting development. We stared at each other, wondering what it all meant. If Janet was here the night of the fire, did she kill Will? If she did, she certainly made a leisurely getaway.

Bryce called everyone to get settled, and as usual, almost everyone ignored him, chatting in corners and fussing with their seating arrangements. Two folks were trying to get the coffeemaker going as a couple of other grumpy people stood nearby with empty cups. I peered around for anything resembling a pink bakery box, or a plate of Spitzbuben, but no such luck today. Bryce yelled louder and more shrilly. A few people shot him annoyed looks, but no one sat down. Then Raymond stood up and cleared his throat, and we all hurried over and took our places.

The circle had filled in while I'd been whispering with Graciela and Helen. The usual people who wouldn't miss a party were there, including Ernie and Alice, Marla, and Freda. Even Randy's mother Catherine was there, looking pale, stressed, and about as worn out as the single mother of three, who also holds down a full-time job outside of the home, can look. Her toddler dozed fitfully in her lap. Seeing her reminded me I needed to find a way to track down Randy sometime today and find out what he wanted to tell me.

Raymond cleared his throat again. In a deep, sonorous voice he started. "I believe I'd like to begin this morning with a brief moment of silence for the deceased, if it was Will, or if it was someone else..."

"Oh, it was Will," someone hissed on the other side of the circle. I cut my eyes over there but couldn't tell if it was Nina or Helen who had spoken, or maybe someone else altogether. Raymond glanced that way too, then went on.

"Whoever it was, we should show respect," he finished. We all lowered our heads. For a few moments the wooden floor stopped creaking and the rustling of people shifting around quieted. The only movements were dust motes circling in beams of morning sunlight streaming through the streaked windows. The spell was broken by little Shawn's frustrated whines as he struggled to get off Catherine's lap. Raymond eased himself down into his battered folding chair and Bryce popped out of his.

"Because of the sad events the last couple of days, we're going to do a check-in, so, and, well, I guess I should start because I have some very strong feelings and..." Bryce launched into a long story about the first time he met Will.

I groaned inwardly, while at the same time exercising tense conscious control over my facial expression. Check-in is where we go around the circle and each person takes as long as they feel they need to take to say whatever they want to say about whatever occurs to them. Interruption is not permitted. A strange thing often occurs when people who have nothing to say are given a captive audience. They talk. For the passive-aggressive amongst us, and there are many, check-in becomes a license to hold other people hostage. With thirty-some people in the room, each one taking anywhere from two to thirty minutes to check-in we could be here for—well, the math should be obvious.

Glancing up from my reverie, I saw Bryce glaring at me. Belatedly, I realized he had said something to me, or maybe about me. In either case, passive-aggressive types hate it when they are not getting the attention to which they feel entitled. I changed my expression from pokerfaced to friendly-attentive and nodded.

"And also," he went on, "dogs are not allowed inside the roadhouse. That is strictly against the rules. And um, I feel...I feel...," he searched for an approved feeling word that would not make him look weak and wimpy. He finally went with, "...violated when people break the rules." I nodded again. Rebutting or defending oneself is not permitted during check-in. Anyway, I could certainly imagine that Bryce did feel violated when other people broke rules. Bryce's world is black and white. There are clear lines between bad and good, between right and wrong. What makes something wrong are rules against it. There are no shades of gray, no extenuating circumstances, no conditions under which it might be okay to ignore the rules. When rules are ignored, Bryce feels violated. I nodded again in understanding of his world view. "I feel pain at the loss of a friend. I feel..." he searched for a word again, "... anguish. I feel sorrow, deep, deep sorrow." Bryce paused and looked around, "And I'd like the right to have the floor again later to finish my check-in. I have so much more I need to say, I need to be heard, and it is, it is so hard to find the words." He turned his gaze and his appeal toward Raymond.

It isn't really up to Raymond when or how long each of us has to speak at check-in, but the deep furrow between his eyebrows revealed that he was having one of his I've-had-it-with-all-of-you people, mornings.

"This isn't the Senate, Bryce. You can't filibuster and you can't check-in twice. Thelma?"

By starting around the circle in this direction, Raymond probably saved us all a good half hour. There was a sudden angry huff of air from Amanita, who, sitting on the other side of Bryce, was all geared up for a good, long, scalding check-in. She was indignant. To let her know I'd noticed that she'd let her poker face slip, I shot her a shocked and angry frown.

"Excuse me?" Catherine was politely interrupting. "Somebody said this was a meeting about the fire? Informational, you know?" More quietly, she mumbled to those around her, "I haven't slept much the last two nights, and I've got laundry to catch up on."

"Amen to that," someone echoed, and similar rumblings came from around the circle. I nodded slightly but did not make eye contact with anyone. As if on cue, Shiner came around and laid his head softly in my lap. He rolled his brown eyes up to mine with a long look that could only mean, "Let's get the heck out of here and go play with a stick." I stroked his head. My sentiments exactly.

"Excuse me!" Bryce said, his voice rising. "This meeting is about feelings, about how we feel, about how I feel! This meeting is to help deal with feelings. This meeting is about me and my family and my feelings!"

Catherine nodded, then quietly said, "Oh."

Perfect opportunity to get up and leave, right? I shot Helen a look, and she at me, but nobody moved. How incredibly callous would it look to leave at that moment? What kind of repercussions would it have if I left now? Maybe tomorrow I would need some help with something from someone here. Who among this community would be there to help me then, if I got up and left this meeting now? Looking down, I rubbed Shiner's head again.

Thelma asked why we couldn't all love each other and get along like a family. Nina and I turned our completely expressionless faces to one another from across the circle. Both Nina and I come from large extended families: hers from central Mexico near León, mine Mexican on my father's side and Irish Catholic on my mother's side. We've talked about some decidedly unloving and unhappy experiences with family. Although both of my parents have passed on to a happier place, what's left of my father's Mexican family still doesn't speak to what's left of my mother's Irish family. No one, it seems, could accept my parents' mixed marriage, and the wisdom of each family's disapproval was proven by the fact that for the first sixteen years of their marriage my parents remained childless. My arrival late in their childbearing years could not have been a bigger surprise, although, I hasten to add, neither could it have been a happier one, at least to my way of thinking.

I hear every day in my counseling practice about not-so-joyful families. From my perspective, turning Arroyo Loco into one big family was not guaranteed to be the boundless joy Thelma seemed to believe. Anyway, after going on in this vein for a time, and being handed a tissue by Betsy, who looked stoically at the floor through Thelma's pleas, she finally wound down.

We shifted our attention to Betsy. She sat completely still until the slightest shuffle or change of position in the room had ceased. On a long intake of breath, she drew herself up and rolled her eyes heavenward, a slight and beatific smile on her lips. As she opened her mouth to speak, Thomas gave the tiniest of coughs. Betsy's eyes narrowed, her head snapped down and she sent a glare across the circle that was so hot with anger, honestly, it seemed Thomas would explode into flames.

"I feel lost," Betsy started, in a voice meant to sound dreamy and far away, but instead, sounded tight and angry. "I miss the trust and the caring that I so longingly seek in this community. I feel, more than ever, that no one is looking after me." She paused and looked around for some sympathetic nods and did get a couple. "For those of you who knew...for those of you who bothered to know..." here she shot pointed glares to a select few, including yours truly, "... my surgery went well last week. Given enough time, I should make a full recovery." She looked around again to gauge the effect of her words. I caught her husband Dick, who sat next to her, giving an almost imperceptible forbidden eye roll. Being one of those who had not bothered to know, I was baffled.

From the corner of my eye, I caught Helen leaning far forward in her chair. She had a look of complete and utter incredulity on her face, which only increased when she caught my glance. Her accompanying gesture expressed that perhaps Betsy had had hangnail surgery? Unable to control a grin, I turned it on Shiner and stroked his head lovingly, maybe a little too hard, until I could regain a stoic expression.

When I looked up, Betsy was glaring back and forth between Helen and me. Really! What did I do? She started in again, using herself as an example of how Arroyo Loco residents treat each other in uncaring ways and complaining that her efforts to help others often went unacknowledged.

As she droned on, I wondered about the intense need some people have to be seen and thanked by others. Maybe we all have that need. I flashed back to an essay I read once by James Thurber in which he comically suggested that we all go about our day by occasionally saying to friends or even complete strangers, "Thank you!" Or maybe it was "I'm sorry!" or "Congratulations!" I can't remember. In any case, it was Thurber's contention that everyone is walking around feeling like they have never been adequately thanked, or apologized to, or congratulated for their accomplishments. Thus, upon hearing a thank you, even from a complete stranger, almost everyone will respond with heartfelt, grateful appreciation. And we've all heard the sentiment, popularized by Maya Angelou, that people may not remember the words you said, but they do remember how you made them feel. Saying thank you, earnestly and often, will generate enormous goodwill. The only thing that beats it is a sincere, I'm sorry.

My attention was drawn to Betsy not by any words she was saying, but more by some strange heat/energy thing she was directing at me. Uh-oh. Biggest crime of all is appearing to ignore Betsy. She was glaring at me in pure hatred. And silence. I felt like the proverbial deer in the headlights, since I had not an inkling of what she'd said.

Raymond jumped in, "Okay, thank you Betsy. Dick?"

Now white hot, Betsy said, "I wasn't finished, Raymond."

"Oh," he replied, seemingly impervious to her fury. "Could you wrap it up?"

By now it was hard to say who Betsy's anger was most directed toward. I think even Dick's eye roll had not gone unnoticed. In a tight and angry snarl, she finished. "I only wanted to say that any dogs running loose in our pristine park area may soon find something very unhealthy for them there."

There was a moment of shocked silence around the circle. Was Betsy threatening to poison dogs? In the park where children played?

Helen, of course Helen, broke the silence. "Wow," she said, "you really are a bitch, aren't you?"

Nobody moved; nobody made a sound. It was all on Helen now, and nobody was going to take any action that might be interpreted as agreement or disagreement, including me, I am embarrassed to say. Then, from somewhere on that side of the circle came a faint whisper, "Witch, Helen, witch!"

Too angry to move, Betsy stared straight ahead as her lips tightened and her face turned redder and redder. When I glanced that way a few minutes later, tears were running down her freckled cheeks.

Dick cleared his throat and jumped into the silence. A proud veteran of the war in Vietnam, Dick is also a filled-with-hot-air know-it-all who is always trying to bully projects ahead before they are fully thought out. He and Will almost came to blows at one meeting when Dick was trying to get the construction of a workshop approved. It was an appropriate location next to the fire engine garage but, due to Will's vehement opposition, the project was not approved. Dick has never fully recovered from his fury. His feelings this morning were chiefly concerned with the risk to property values posed by the burned wreckage of the Rosenblums' house. His not-unfounded belief was that the HOA would probably argue about the cleanup until the mess rotted. He concluded his remarks by proposing a new rule requiring the timely clean up and repair of any structures in Arroyo Loco that burn down.

Nearly all the men here are retired or otherwise unable or unwilling to be gainfully employed, leading to a situation where too many of them have a good deal too much time on their hands. Dick Carper is a good example.

Finding no other way to stay occupied, these guys have formed various HOA committees and enjoy pestering the rest of us with endless mandatory meetings and new rules for everything from parking to what kinds of fences we can build.

We skipped a few empty seats and got to Raymond, who asked us to let the sheriff do his job, and to look out for each other when we could without intruding on each other. As usual, Raymond shared nothing about his own feelings, which seemed to range on a single dimension from tense to relaxed. At the moment, he was tense.

Another empty seat and we got to Sunshine. I wondered if she and Raymond leave an empty seat between them in hopes of diffusing any rumors about their affections for one another? A psychologist is never not working, never not wondering about motivations, interactions, and relationship dynamics.

The contributions thus far had been uniformly negative, bordering on downright nasty. I was curious to hear how Sunshine would spin the events of the last day and a half. She stared resolutely at her hands, then began. "I would like us all to focus on the positive. It is a beautiful morning," she said as she looked reverently through the dusty but sunny window. "I would like us all to appreciate those loving individuals who surround us at this moment. I would like us to share in the joy of having one another here this morning to talk to, and to care about each other in loving ways. I would like us to bring the positive into our lives and our community, to focus on our intention to live in appreciation of one another, and allow the positive to manifest itself in our lives and in our community." Classic

Sunshine. Nothing about her feelings; lots about abstract concepts straight out of the latest self-help book.

A quick shuffle behind us, and Delia slipped into the chair on the other side of Raymond. This morning she had taken special care with her hair and makeup. Her lipstick perfectly matched the bright maroon of her Lycra leotard. A chartreuse broomstick-style skirt swirled around her shins. She gave Raymond a simpering look of apology and batted her mascara-laden lashes at him.

"Mornin' Raymond," she crooned.

Without moving one facial muscle, Sunshine leaned slightly over in my direction and whispered hotly, "Hoo-chee-mama!"

"Oh, and, by the way," Delia continued, this time addressing everyone, "Just now, I came down by way of Wally's driveway, and his car smells like some fool poured gasoline all over the trunk!"

There was a moment of silence. Then Ernie called out matter-of-factly, "Well, it is a car. They're supposed to smell of gasoline."

Nobody had a rebuttal to that. Then it was my turn to check-in. I had long considered how much I should say in this very public setting. Generally, these are not people one wants to share one's feelings with, but I've learned the hard way that I can't get away forever with saying I'm fine. So, I said I was nervous. Nervous is a feeling, right? "And," I said, "until we know what happened Friday night, and how that fire got started, my dogs are not going to be left alone even for a few minutes. They take care of me, and I take care of them." I stroked Shiner's head. He gave me one of those long, loving gazes that not even a concerned psychotherapist can match, as if to say the feeling was mutual. I looked around and smiled benignly at the ugly little pug piled on pillows in Margaret's ample lap, including all dogs in my moment of Zen. The virtual check-in baton then passed to Catherine, sitting to my right.

Catherine quickly said she was scared and she hoped we would all do what Raymond said and let the sheriff do his job. Little Shawn slapped at her chin as she talked, giggling as she tried to swat his hand away. As soon as she finished talking, she gathered him up in his blanket and slipped out of the circle.

Next, Graciela said she was concerned. She didn't look concerned, but that's what she said. She then announced that she had an open house from noon to four o'clock today at a lovely three bedroom cottage on the western edge of Atascadero with easy access to shopping, schools, and medical care. Everyone was welcome to drop by and take a look around. There was the slightest hint that we might especially like to view the property if we were thinking at all about escaping the madness of Arroyo Loco. Graciela concluded her announcement with a brilliant and inviting smile. She turned expectantly to Sofia.

Sofia sat stiffly, staring straight ahead at some indeterminate point on the floorboards, her arms wrapped tightly around her thin body. Her eyes flicked briefly to her mother. Then she gave the kind of an eye roll that only a pre-adolescent can give, and shifted to turn slightly away from Graciela with a horrified look and a shudder. I was only guessing, but thinking Sofia did not want to check-in that morning.

It was Helen's turn. She started by telling us about the damage to her cat cage, and the missing, possibly kidnapped cat, Mocha. In a surprisingly calm voice, she went on to say that she heard a red-tailed hawk screaming across the canyon early this morning, and assumed that Mocha had gone the way of breakfast for the hawk. My stomach lurched and we all had another spontaneous moment of silence. In the same calm voice, Helen added that she felt infuriated, and that she intended to find the party responsible for cutting the hole in her cat cage. No word on what would happen after that.

Next in the circle, Freda announced her hope that Will's house would be rebuilt soon because it was an eyesore. It was worse than her dead magnolia, she added, with the merest suggestion of a smile. Then she turned to Nina.

Like most of us, Nina was in her public persona, with her hands folded demurely in her lap. "I'm fine," she started. "I hope for the sake of the children we can clear this all up and clean up that burned area soon." Since when were the children a big priority with Nina? She smiled angelically and turned to Margaret and her pug in the wheelchair to Nina's right. The pug lifted his head, then his lip, and growled menacingly. Nina shifted slightly away.

The next several people expressed similar sentiments of sorrow, mixed with fear and concern about the arsonist. Margaret voiced regret that she hadn't gotten to know Will better. Several of us struggled with the eye rolling prohibition over that one.

There were more empty chairs in that section. Lauren and Valerie were missing; no surprise there. In fact, a fair number of residents were not in attendance at this so-called mandatory meeting.

When it was Marla's turn, she said she was curious about what had really happened at Will's house. I don't like Marla, and I most definitely don't trust her, but she was the only one to admit to being curious, although I know we all were, so I had to give her that one.

Sitting on the metal folding chair next to Marla was the tape recorder. For a moment, we all stared at it whirring quietly away there. Why were Tina and Wally recording this meeting? Patting Shiner's head again, I was glad the dogs were with me and not home alone.

CHAPTER TEN

We shifted our collective attention to the next chair, where Tina was huddled. From behind the drape of lackluster hair, her tremulous voice emerged. "Arroyo Loco is a dangerous place!" She stopped. There was a sudden silence. After a few seconds, someone on the right shifted in their chair, the floor creaked, and Tina quietly repeated, "Arroyo Loco is a dangerous place. There are treacherous people here. We should all be very careful." It was impossible to decipher whether her tone was meant to sound threatening, or if she was simply fearful herself. We all sat reflecting on that for a bit. After a few seconds of silence, Tina muttered that she would pass, which Ernie had to repeat because no one on our side of the circle could hear her.

From my perspective, it looked as though Wally was still focused across the circle on me. Still with the creepy smirk. I couldn't tell if he was thinking about making a sandwich or stabbing me in the eye with an ice pick. After a heartbeat he murmured "pass" and shifted his gaze to the floor.

Then it was Alice's turn. The usual goofy grin lighted Alice's face, completely incongruent with the prevailing mood, and, as it turned out, with what she was about to say. She looked around the circle nervously. Under her breath she whispered, "Yes, yes," several times, kind of working her way up to a speaking voice.

Ernie broke in, "We got a phone call this morning," he paused, "from Janet." Around the circle there were gasps. Attention was suddenly riveted to Ernie. "I'll let Alice tell you all about it. She took the call." He turned to Alice expectantly, as did the rest of us. At last, the whole story would be told. We were on the edges of our seats.

"Yes, yes," Alice started again, her voice shaking. "Janet called me this morning. I've already told the police. She called. She said she and Kenneth arrived at about eight or eight-thirty Friday evening to get her things. She's leaving Will. She didn't want to move here in the first place and he's more and more controlling and after thirty-five years of waiting on him hand and foot...." She shot a pointed look in Ernie's direction. Ernie made a let's-get-on-with-this rolling motion with his hand, and Alice flashed him another quick angry glance. "Yes, yes," she said. "Kenneth isn't really sick. Janet needed him to come help her get her things. He's not really sick, it was all just a...a..." She turned to Ernie searching for the word she wanted.

"A ruse, a trick," he said loudly, "a game, a way to get Will to let her go...."

"Yes, yes," Alice interrupted, "...a ruse. Anyway they got home and found Will in his bed. She said he was sleeping and they couldn't wake him up."

From somewhere to the right of me I heard that cynical voice again, "So she says." Had to be Helen. I didn't look.

"Janet said she sat with him a while. She didn't want him to wake up anyway, you know, because she was leaving. She left some letters by his side as a way of saying goodbye, Kenneth put his own ring on Will, as a token of respect...."

"More likely to confuse the police." That voice again.

Alice sent a tight-lipped frown across the circle. "Janet was really crying. She was shocked to hear about the fire, and the...you know...." Tears spilled generously down Alice's own cheeks. She wasn't the only one here weeping. Sunshine pulled a packet of tissues out of the tapestry bag by her feet, took one, handed one to Raymond, and passed the rest to me. Hmm, guess I didn't need one. I sent them on around.

"Did she know for sure he was sleeping?" Sunshine asked in a gentle tone.

"Yes, yes," Alice started. "Well, I don't know. That's what she told me. Maybe he had a heart attack. She said she couldn't see anything wrong with him. He was lying there peacefully asleep."

"Janet's not coming home," Ernie jumped in. "She and Kenneth are gone to Mexico and that's where they're staying."

"Okay, that sounds suspicious." Helen's voice again. "Why are they running off to Mexico if they didn't kill Will? Did they pour the gasoline, or at least smell it around the house?"

"Janet?" someone else whispered incredulously.

Alice's eyes got big as she stared at Helen. "Janet didn't say anything about gasoline. I guess they didn't smell anything."

That seemed to be about all Alice had to say regarding her conversation with Janet. Her revelations almost raised more questions than they answered. Then it was Ernie's turn. This should be brief, as, like a lot of guys, Ernie was either mad or mellow.

"What I want to know," he said, "is who is getting into our ice cream in the freezer? I go out and buy all this ice cream for our Wednesday potluck, and this morning half of it has been eaten already! Including the pistachio, which hardly anybody even likes!" There was silence around the circle as we collectively recovered from cognitive whiplash.

Raymond was as puzzled as the rest of us. "Someone's getting into the freezer here in the roadhouse and eating the ice cream?" he confirmed.

"Yes!" Ernie almost screeched, his indignation growing stronger, "And I want to know who it is!"

"The freezer is locked, right? Only HOA board members have keys?"

"Yes!"

There was general mumbling around the circle and several potential villains were offered up including, "It's those damn kids again," and, inexplicably, "Wally!"

"Could we get back to the subject, please!" Bryce called loudly.

"Oh, well." Helen, in a hoarse whisper again. Uh-oh. "Back to the subject, please. How does Brycie feel about the disappearing ice cream?" Helen may offend many people for obvious reasons, but she can also be counted on for a laugh now and again.

From the corner of my eye, I shot a look at Amanita, last in the circle to talk. She was furious that our check-in had gotten derailed and was threatening to become a general conversation before she had her turn. Her face was the precise color and texture of an extremely over-ripe heirloom tomato, about ready to burst.

I yawned in as inconspicuous a way as possible, then glanced in the direction of the sunny east window of the meeting room. I wished the dogs and I could be out there enjoying the beautiful morning. Nina wiggled her eyebrows at me and looked demurely around the circle to see if anyone had noticed. So far, so good. Ever so slightly, she inclined her head toward the door and gave me a long stare. The message was clear. If we snuck out now, we could avoid the minimum of half an hour that it would take for Amanita to tell everyone how she was feeling that morning. I gently nudged the now-sleeping Shiner with the toe of my shoe. He leapt up from his nap and shook his collar and tags loudly, garnering several nasty glares. He stared pointedly at me. No need for raised eyebrows to read his expression. With murmured apologies, I rose and slipped between the chairs, gathering up towels and leashes as I went. Glancing sideways, I saw Nina standing up to help Margaret get her wheelchair turned around, the pug snarling quietly. Nina was trying to keep out of snapping range. A few seconds later, Thomas and his mother met us on the porch, and between us we got her down the steep ramp Dick had constructed after a lengthy and laborious HOA approval process.

"I wonder if when people get up and leave a boring meeting because their baby is crying, do you suppose they have pinched the baby to make him cry?" I said.

Thomas gave an agreeable grunt. Nina looked like she was doing calisthenics with her eye balls, but she was probably loosening them up for reuse after the enforced inactivity of the HOA meeting.

We strolled toward Nina's place next door alongside Thomas pushing Margaret. The pug was now standing on

Margaret's lap, making seriously threatening noises at Scout and Shiner. They politely ignored the much smaller dog.

"Say, Thomas, I've been wanting to ask you something," I said, to which he grunted affirmatively. I've rarely heard him speak actual words, but he can use grunts remarkably effectively. "You, Ernie, and Wally were together in the roadhouse on Friday night when the fire alarm went off, right?"

"Uh-huh."

"So, what time did you get there that night?"

Margaret piped up here in her scratchy voice. "They always go at eight on Friday nights. Ernie has the key. He comes by at eight, and Thomas goes down with him, and then whoever else meets them there. That's why Thomas went out Friday night in his bedroom slippers. He wasn't quite ready when Ernie came by."

"So, Wally joined you there that night?"

"Uh-huh."

"What time did Wally did get there? Did Wally get there the same time you got there on Friday night?"

"Uh-uh."

"So, he got there after you did? Or before you?"

"Uh-huh."

"After you got there he came in?"

"Uh-huh."

"Right away after you got there? Shortly after you got there?

"Uh-huh"

"So, Wally got there a few minutes after you got the place unlocked?"

"Yup, five minutes, most!" Thomas smiled proudly and folded his pudgy hands across his belly. That was quite a speech for him.

The pug was really snarling by that time, so Thomas and Margaret pushed off again, heading for their place. Nina called after them, "Margaret, I'll bring that strudel recipe to you later today!" Margaret sent a little wave in acknowledgement. I slipped my dogs into Nina's yard through the gate, and she and I settled in on the stylish decorator porch furniture, where Helen joined us a few minutes later.

"Okay, well, holy cow!" Helen exhaled as she climbed the wide steps. "That was exciting. I was sure Betsy was going to lynch me."

"She still might," Nina said.

"But she is such a witch! I don't know why the rest of you put up with her at all."

"Yeah, well, sometimes she's not so bad," I said out loud, thinking about how Betsy helped me yesterday. "How did you sneak out of the meeting? Isn't Amanita livid that so many of us left before she got to share her feelings?"

"She was probably glad to see me go," Helen said. "She has the floor completely to herself now, and there are fewer rolling eyes and raised eyebrows in the room."

"I was never clear," Nina mused, "I know eye rolling is not permitted, but is there also a rule against raising eyebrows?"

All we could do was shake our heads over that one and smile. "Well, if there isn't a rule about that now, there soon will be," Helen remarked. "Okay, are they going to talk about the fire at all, or was this strictly a check-in meeting?" None of us knew any more than the others on that one.

"What are you thinking about the fire and all, now that we've heard from Janet?" Helen asked. "I mean, now we know that Janet was here, and she said Will was in his bed and already dead by eight thirty that night, way before the fire started."

"No, she said he was asleep," said Nina.

Another dubious grunt from Helen. "So she said. But of course she would say that if she killed him, or maybe drugged him, and still hopes the fire destroyed all the evidence."

"No, really Helen, think about it," I started. "If Janet killed Will, why would she casually stop by Graciela's as she was leaving town?"

"Janet couldn't kill anyone." Nina added. "She weighs about 90 pounds dripping wet, and is as weak as a...as a..."

"A kitten," Helen finished, nodding.

"She could have drugged him," I said, "or someone else could have drugged him." I was looking at Helen. "Remember, Delia's a home health nurse. She probably has access to drugs. But she left too early to have started the fire. And Janet did too," I finished.

"So who did start the fire?" Nina asked.

"Estela and I think Valerie snuck across and torched Will's place," Helen asserted.

"Well, maybe." I shook my head. "That's a long way for a woman in her fifties to haul a full five gallon can without being seen. Would being pissed off at Will be enough of a motive? Where was Lauren while Valerie was off committing arson?" Nobody had any answers.

"Thomas says Wally was down at the roadhouse by about five minutes after eight at the latest," I said. "So, as much as we might want it to be him, he didn't start the fire." Shaking my head, I considered the incriminating bucket in my driveway. So far, no one else had said anything about the bucket, and my strange conversation with Tina last night remained unshared. I felt awkward about bringing it up, so decided to keep it to myself.

"Okay, Wally was in the roadhouse from eight o'clock until the alarm went off? He didn't leave until the fire alarm went off?" Helen asked. I nodded, and she went on, "Well, maybe he poured the gasoline and someone else started the fire."

"Ooh," Nina whispered. "Yes, like, he had an accomplice?"

"Yeah," Those kids and their cigarettes again. "Or someone else came along and accidentally lit the fire."

"Accidentally lit the fire?" Nina raised her eyebrows skeptically.

"So, let's back up for a minute here," I said. "I know we hate him, and Wally does have a good motive, but why are you assuming it had to be Wally who poured the gasoline? For that matter, how did Will die? Janet told Alice that Will was sleeping when she got here, but, like Helen said before, how do we know she's telling the truth? Seems like Janet and Kenneth had the best opportunity to kill him and start the fire." I stuck up three fingers and counted off, "Means, motive, opportunity."

"Everybody had opportunity," Helen said. "As for motive, Wally, Janet, Valerie, and Delia had the best motives." She paused. "You already said we have to wait to find out the means of death."

"Yeah, although it wasn't anything too gory, so probably not a gun or a knife," I speculated.

"Now, wait a second! Not everyone had opportunity. I couldn't possibly carry five gallons of gasoline all the way over there," Nina asserted. "Let's go into town, get a five gallon can, and fill it. I'll show you! I wouldn't be able to pick it up. C'mon let's go right now! Macy's is having a white sale today only anyway." Nina does have a gentle way of lightening a mood. "Anyway, I mean," she went on, "the body was cremated, and so was all the evidence. He was peacefully lying there. I'm going to pretend death was by natural causes, and that's all I want to hear on the subject."

Helen and I shot each other sideways looks, then nodded thoughtfully.

"In which case, it wasn't murder at all," Helen added. "Unless he was drugged." Another round of raised eyebrows. I know it happens on television all the time, but that seemed a little dramatic and far-fetched for Arroyo Loco.

"If the point wasn't to kill Will, then what was the point of burning the house?" Nina asked.

We looked at each other and said, in unison, "The photographs!"

"Yes! So it was Wally who poured the gasoline and started the fire!" concluded Nina.

"Well, Nina," Helen complained, "the fire started between eight forty-five and nine, and Wally was in the roadhouse beginning at five minutes after eight. So, how does he start the fire? Does he leave the roadhouse, go up to Will's, start the fire and run down to the roadhouse without anyone seeing him?" For emphasis, she made the scurrying motions with her fingers again, like Nina did yesterday.

"Yes, he did," Nina declared. "Only I don't know how he did that."

Finally, a light went on upstairs. "Ah-ha! That one, I think I do have an answer for," I announced. "There's a trail."

"A trail?"

"Yeah. Actually, a whole network of trails. They run along the ridge back there." Standing up, I pointed. "And then down and across, and over down behind Thomas's, and probably back along behind here too."

Helen stood up too, searching the hillside beyond Nina's fenced area. "I don't see anything."

"You can't see any of the trails from here. Most of the time you can't see when people are on the trails. They're hidden behind rocks and brush. That's kind of the point. The kids, and whoever else, can travel all around this canyon and never be seen." By now, Nina was standing up looking too. "What's more, spurs go off the main trail to places where you can see into almost everyone's rear windows."

"Really!" Nina whispered.

Helen was scowling. "Okay, that's how they snuck around and cut my cat cage without being seen, isn't it?"

"Well, not the kids I don't think, but that's probably how someone got there without being seen," I agreed. "And I also found the place where those pictures of Wally and Sofia were taken. It's on the spur that comes down toward your house."

"Who else knows about those trails, Estela?" Nina whispered again, as though we were sharing a secret.

"Hmm. I suppose most anyone could know about them. I only know because the kids were out there yesterday morning, and later I went exploring." After a few more seconds I said, "Will had to know. He was convinced those kids were up to no good and was always trying to catch them at something."

"Yes. Maybe that's what Sunshine means when she says our negative thoughts manifest in negative events in our lives," suggested Nina.

We pondered that briefly, then simultaneously, Helen and I laughed, "Who knows what Sunshine means!"

"Anyway, I'm sure Will knew because one of the main gathering places is right behind his house. That's how I got onto the trail yesterday. But other than him," I paused, "anyone could know."

"Well, Bryce didn't seem surprised to see the kids out there yesterday," said Helen. I had to agree with that. "So, Bryce knows about the trail."

"Yes. And you think that's how Wally got down here to the roadhouse without being seen on Friday night?" Nina asked.

"Yeah, that might be how he did it."

"Okay, Bryce knows about them." Helen began to enumerate, "Bryce, the kids, Will, Wally, and we don't know who else. So who cut my cat cage yesterday? Will was dead. The kids helped me round up Custard, so I don't think they did it. That leaves Wally or Bryce."

"Or person or persons unknown," Nina pointed out.

"Somebody's watching too many crime shows," I joked.

"Okay, why? Why would someone do that?" Helen was still lost in her own drama and her beleaguered cats.

"You know, Helen," I began, "You do have a tendency to offend people sometimes."

"What?" she exclaimed righteously. "I only say what's true!"

"Yeah," I agreed. "That's probably correct, but still, you can be a bit insensitive."

She grunted again empathically. "I only say the same thing the rest of you are thinking!"

"Yeah, that's almost always true," I agreed again. "But I'm only suggesting, maybe what you say sometimes offends some people."

"Well," she continued indignantly, "they should get a thicker skin. Or get a life. Or...or get something..."

"I think what Estela's trying to say, Helen, is what they're getting is a handy set of bolt cutters," said Nina.

We all sat down and considered that for a while. The roadhouse meeting appeared to be breaking up as a few more neighbors wandered by Nina's porch. Freda let herself in the gate and plopped into the only empty chair left. Gazing across the road toward Thelma's tiny house, I focused on Thelma herself rocking rapidly on her shady front porch. Too far away to see her expression, her body and the steady rocking spoke of barely controlled fury. "What's up with Thelma?" I asked my friends. Nina shifted that direction and waved brightly toward Thelma. She got no response. Helen turned and scowled, then shook her head and said nothing. Another mystery in Arroyo Loco.

"Speaking of Wally," Helen started in again. "What's his story? I mean, how does a person get that sick and twisted? Was he born a bad seed?"

"Oh, no!" Freda exclaimed seriously. "It was his mother. She did not raise him right. She mistreated him!" Her eyes grew wide, but there were enough mothers sitting here to know she was being sarcastic.

"That's a fairly common assumption, isn't it Freda?" I joined in her riff. "But all mothers make mistakes now and then, moments of impatience, frustration, and not all kids turn out to be homicidal maniacs and pedophiles."

This earned me three horrified stares. Maybe I should work on my delivery. Or maybe there were more homicidal maniacs among the kids in our lives than I knew.

"Now, really, Estela, you're the expert. You are the psychologist," Nina said, still very serious. "Why do most boys grow up to be normal husbands and men, to want to, you know, be in relationships with other adults, and then one boy grows up and wants to abuse children?"

A serious question, deserving of a serious answer. "That's a good question, Nina. No one really knows why. The problem with blaming the mother is, the evidence doesn't support that explanation. Some researchers think it has to do with brain chemistry. There's one study that suggests a tumor in a particular place in the brain causes pedophilia."

"I always assumed it was frustration that caused men to go after kids," said Helen. "You know, like all of those Catholic priests who are supposed to be celibate their whole lives? For what reason other than frustration would they do that? They're acting out of frustration."

"What about all of those heterosexual happily married men who become Boy Scout leaders and then molest the boys?" asked Nina.

Freda was puzzled. "If they molest boys, how can they be heterosexual?"

Helen was incensed. "Even though they get all kinds of support from public taxes, the Boy Scouts of America don't allow gay men to be leaders. So their adult members are all heterosexual. And they still have a huge and mostly hidden problem with adult leaders molesting the boys." Clearly, this was a topic Helen knew something about.

"It's true, Freda," I added. "The vast majority of pedophiles are heterosexual men. Many of them say they are happily married to women, and their victims are both boys and girls. The most supported theories suggest that the cause has more to do with domination and control than with anything else. These men have a need to feel powerful and to dominate others. So they molest children and abuse animals. Their actions have very little to do with sex and everything to do with being more powerful than their victims. So, Helen, it's not frustration. It's domination over those less powerful."

We all gazed into space, and a couple of us sighed deeply. Humans. Not my favorite species.

"The other thing about Wally is, in addition to being afraid Tina would leave him, he is also a sociopath. Sociopaths don't experience shame. Wally knows what he did to the girls, for example, was considered wrong, but he felt no guilt or remorse. He did whatever he wanted no matter who it hurt, and figured the rest of us were fools for not doing the same. Wally's only concern was that he didn't want to get caught." We mulled that over. "You know," I concluded, "the only thing we know for sure about pedophiles is that we have to identify them and then get them away from our children."

My growling stomach interrupted the silence that followed. Lunch time. "Got to get going with these dogs," I announced. Helen and Freda walked most of the way with Shiner and Scout and me. Once on the screened porch, the dogs headed for their dog door, then stopped. They both stared intently into the shadow cast on the other side of the storage closet to my right, almost as though they had something cornered there. Shiner let out a soft woof. The fur on the back of his neck stood straight up. Something, or someone, was definitely there. I froze.

We heard a shuffling, then a scraping sound. I watched in horror and the dogs' noses rose upward as the thing in the shadows grew before their eyes. Someone was standing up, and it was a big someone. Also, that someone was a smoker. Not smoking now, but the odor of cigarette smoke lingers for days in clothes, in hair, on the skin. Suddenly, I snapped into action. "What the hell is going on here?" I yelled as loudly and in as deep a voice as I could muster. I don't know why this is my typical reaction in a perceived crisis, or how I would follow up if anything ever turned out to really be a crisis. It must be my natural inclination to put on a strong offense in hopes that my undependable and mostly nonexistent defenses won't be needed. Anyway, by then Shiner was starting to wag his tail and wiggle.

Randy, looking sleepy and somewhat chagrined, stepped out of the shadows. He handed me my precious Giants baseball cap.

"Sorry if I scared you, Miz Estela. My bad again." He lowered his head and shook it slightly. "I fell asleep. I didn't get a lot a sleep last night. We gotta talk. I mean, I gotta talk to you about somethin'." He still didn't look up.

"Yeah?" I replied doubtfully in a shaky voice. Taking a deep breath, I started again. "I'm sorry I yelled. You did kinda scare me." Thinking about it twice, I invited him to sit down in the wicker. "I think I've got some soda. Let's get you one."

"Naw," he replied. "All you got is ginger ale."

Hmm. Startled. Which way to go with this piece of information? Angry or scared that he knows what I have in my refrigerator? Embarrassed that I habitually keep nerdy soda? This couldn't go without comment.

"That's very annoying Randy, to know that you apparently have been in my house when I wasn't home. You know that's the kind of activity that will get you in trouble with the cops again, at the very least. What if you ran into a scared and armed homeowner? You could get shot." Giving him my best stern face, he finally made eye contact.

"I'm not lookin' to get into any more trouble, Miz Estela. You know, you guys don't give us kids any credit. We been keepin' an eye on all'a your houses for a long time. There's homeless guys out there on that trail, and thieves, real thieves, and worse. You should be grateful us kids is out there keepin' a watch out. We see stuff," he paused. "That's what I need to talk to you about."

This sounded serious, and indeed, Randy looked close to tears. On the other hand, it was past my lunch time. Weighing the odds, I invited him into the kitchen. Head-butting their way in behind him, the dogs joined us. I made both Randy and me tuna sandwiches. He turned his nose up at a bowl of homemade butternut squash soup, but my chocolate chip cookies were a hit. We chatted about his friends, how his uncle, stationed in Turkey, was doing, and when and how Randy was going to get a car. Finally we got around to the reason for his unexpected visit.

"Okay, I'm gonna tell you somethin' that might get me in trouble, real trouble. I don't wanna get in trouble, but I gotta tell you because, well, because I gotta tell you somethin' else. Somethin' that's more important."

"I'm listening," I said, leaning forward on the kitchen table. Scout, who had been standing by, waiting for a stray piece of tuna, sidled up and draped his head across Randy's lap. My certified therapy dog going to work. The much younger Shiner, deciding some game must be afoot, brought a disgustingly well-chewed small stuffed bear to Randy and pushed it into his lap. Raising soft-brown hopeful eyes to Randy's, Shiner waited for him to throw it. Like most young herding dogs, Shiner's entire universe revolves around fetching. Randy stroked Scout's head, as his breathing slowed and he calmed. He was clearly more familiar with my dogs than I knew.

"Thing is," he continued cryptically, "can I not get in trouble for the thing I did if I tell you about the thing I saw?"

"You mean you want to buy some kind of immunity for what you did by providing information about something you witnessed?"

He looked at me quizzically for a moment. Too many big words was my guess. Then he nodded, his face still full of doubt. "Yeah," he said slowly, "I think that's what I mean."

Giving up on the bear, Shiner disappeared and returned a few seconds later with a squeaky pink pig toy. He dropped that at Randy's feet and looked expectantly at the boy again.

I'm not a lawyer. I have had some experience advocating for clients in the courtroom, but I'm not qualified to give legal advice. Without more information, it was hard to say what his options might be in this situation.

I do have a friend who is a criminal attorney. Maybe I should call him? There is always Marla. No, bad idea. A tax attorney who can be trusted is probably an oxymoron, especially in the case of Marla.

After some consideration, I decided to wing it for both of us. "Why don't you tell me what you did, and then what you saw? I'll give you my best judgment about whether you need immunity, or if you do, what the odds are that you might get it. How about that?"

He nodded seriously, but didn't say anything.

"That's the best I've got, Randy." I threw up my hands.

"Okay. Okay, but I have to tell you what we saw first."

I smiled encouragingly. By this time, he was getting my full attention.

"It was me and a couple of the guys." He made eye contact. "I don't wanna tell you who."

"That's okay," I assured him.

"Me and a couple of the guys saw Wally sneaking around Will's house. It was just gettin' dark Friday night. We was hangin' in that place on the hill behind the house, you know, under the tree, and we saw Wally sneakin' around. We saw him come outta Will's back door, and go off down the trail."

I answered him silently, my eyes growing wide.

"We was hangin' and watchin'. Nobody said nothin'. Then a few minutes later, here comes Wally, sneakin' along again, and he's got this red, plastic gas can. He pours gasoline all around Will's porch and along the wall under that small window." Randy was gesturing back and forth, making pouring of gasoline motions with one hand.

"Wow," was the best I could manage. "So, then what happened?"

Randy took a deep breath. "You know how I told you we keep an eye on stuff that goes on around here? So, this is bad stuff. This is hella bad stuff."

I was nodding, and starting to feel horrified. Some of us wanted to pin the arson on Wally, but here was eyewitness evidence. "So, what did you do?"

"I's mad, you know. I hate that Wally, anyway." He scowled. "I stood up on that rock, that smaller one, you know, and I called out, like, hey you, what the fuck you doin' down there, motha? and all like that. Scuse my French."

"Yes...?"

"Wally turned in, like, a panic, you know, he's lookin' all around, and he sorta sees me there and he starts calling me all these names, but, like, kinda quiet like he doesn't want anyone to hear him, you know, and then he like runs toward where I am and he pitches that plastic can as far as he can heave it at me, and he's sayin he's gonna burn all us kids up. Then he stops and he says, still kinda quiet like, he says now everyone will think it's us kids that poured the gasoline."

"Wow," I reiterated. "Were you scared?" Randy looked at me like I was nuts.

"No, I wasn't scared! I was mad. I was like hella mad!"

"So, what did you do?"

Then the chagrined look returned. "I was mad, Miz Estela, and when I get mad, I don't think so straight. I mean, here he was tryin' to kill me and my friends. I wasn't thinking about Will's house or anything else. I just went and threw my cigarette at Wally. And I said to him, but real quiet like too, "No, sucka, I'm gonna burn you up." All's I could think about was I was gonna blow Wally up into a big ball a flames. And that it woulda been all his fault cause he's the guy who was pouring the gasoline."

Puzzled, I said, "But nothing happened to him, because I saw him maybe an hour or so later coming out of the roadhouse."

"Naw. My cigarette landed in that green part, the lawn behind Will's. And Wally went runnin' off through the bushes like a scared little girl. We been tryin' to figure out ever since how to get him, cause we are gonna get him. We heard what he done to Sofia." He paused and went on in a very small voice. "And prolly my sister, too."

I leaned back and sighed. "Wow. Randy, that's quite a story."

"Yeah, well, and every word of it is the god's honest truth, too, Miz Estela," he assured me. "I got two witnesses who was with me and who saw everything I saw."

"That's important, Randy. That's a powerful story, and having additional witnesses is important too." I mulled over the details of his tale. "So, what did you do that you think you might need immunity?"

"I throwed that cigarette," he said in a shocked voice. "I started that fire. I mean, it landed in the green part, but it musta gotten to the house after while, cause how else would that fire start? I burned up Will's house and maybe killed Will. I'm in hella lotta trouble." The tears now were spilling, making dirty tracks on his downy cheeks. He swiped at them. "And even if I didn't, someone's gonna say I did. They're gonna lock me up for sure now." Silently, I handed him a tissue from the box conveniently located on the kitchen table. Psychotherapists should buy stock in tissue companies before going into practice.

While he wiped his nose, I gave his story some thought. Randy was worried the lit cigarette he threw at Wally had ignited the fire, but that seemed unlikely to me. Randy threw the cigarette sometime before 8:00 p.m., while Wally was still behind Will's house. The fire was unlikely to have been ignited until more like right before 9:00 p.m. If Wally was down in the roadhouse by the time the fire blew up, and had been there since 8:00 p.m., Wally was absolved of igniting the fire. For the same reason, Randy was also absolved. The timing was all wrong. Don't try this at home, but if gasoline is poured on an old, framed structure and a match tossed on it, or maybe a lit cigarette, it's going to be an instant explosion, not a long drawn out affair that provides ample time to walk down to the local pub, open a bottle, and have a sip or two before the alarm is called. True, the fire at Will's house may, for some reason, have been slow to get started, but there was no evidence to indicate that had been the case.

A plastic Whiffle ball bounced on the floor by Randy's feet. Shiner was still trying to find something that would entice Randy to throw it.

"Randy, what time was it when you saw Wally around the rear of Will's house?"

"Dunno Miz Estela. It was gettin' dark. Like around seven thirty or seven?"

Hmm. Delia and her kids had taken off for her sister's at about 6:00 p.m. Janet and Kenneth left the house at 8:30 p.m. We don't know when they arrived at the house, but Janet's story is that Will was asleep when they arrived. Or maybe they found him dead, and they laid him out in the bed? We might never know which. Anyway, the dogs and I walked past the house at about 8:45 p.m., and there were no signs of a fire then. I would almost certainly have seen something if the fire had started by then. My dogs even ran behind the house there for a minute or two, and other than maybe chasing something, they didn't seem alarmed about anything.

"And what did you guys do after you threw the cigarette and Wally went running off?"

"We went up to that place where you were yesterday, the cave. You know how it is, Miz Estela. Us kids is always gettin' blamed for everything bad that happens around here. We went up there and started tryin' to figure out what we should do. We was gonna tell someone about the gasoline and Wally, and about him being in Will's house. We was trying to figure out who to tell, without someone jumpin' to conclusions and us gettin' blamed for the whole mess. We didn't know nothin' about ole Will being in there dead. And the fire hadn'a started by then neither, so we didn't call no one. I stayed out there all night on accounta I figured Wally was gonna come after me. And yesterday, he did. He was out there lookin' for me. That's why we had that trail booby trapped, and that's why you fell. Sooner or later, he's gonna get me." More quietly, he added, "Or I'm gonna hafta get him." He stared forlornly down at Scout's head as he stroked the dog. "Ya know Miz Estela, I know I done some, like, really dumb stuff in my time, but I'm not, like, you know, totally stupid."

CHAPTER ELEVEN

"I know. I know," I tried to reassure Randy. He was one of those kids who, right from the start, could never seem to catch a break. "For whatever it's worth, in my opinion, there's no way your cigarette could have started that fire. I walked past there at about a quarter to nine and there was no fire then. Even if you threw the cigarette as late as eight o'clock, it would have been long dead by the time that fire got started."

He looked up at me warily, as if to check my trustworthiness. "Really?"

"Yes, Randy, really. If you want, I'll go down there and check. I'll betcha we'll find your cold dead cigarette butt lying there in the middle of the green lawn, yards from where the fire started."

Randy's face began to relax. The last of his tears spilled, this time more in relief, and he gave me a faint smile.

"So, how long were you guys up behind Will's house, and what else did you see? Did you see anything else? What time did you get there?"

"Oh, man, I'm sorry Miz Estela, we really didn't see nothin' else. We just got there. The lights was all off in Will's. That was strange. We was lightin' up, and hadn't sat down yet. That's really the only reason we saw Wally sneakin' out Will's door, cause we wasn't sittin' down yet. Then we heard him comin' back a little later with the gas can, so then we stood up and watched him pour it around. Then him and me, we had our argument, then we all took off. You know, that hadda be before eight, cause…" he paused. "Cause one of us hadda be home by eight. He's grounded and his mom does a bed check every hour. He hadda get in his window by eight."

This was beginning to look worse and worse for Wally. The last anyone saw of Will alive was when he was almost run down in Delia's driveway at around 6:00 p.m. Janet says he was out cold at 8:30 p.m., but we don't know if he was asleep or already dead. Randy and his friends place Wally inside Will's house sometime between 7:00 p.m. and a little before 8:00 p.m. And it wasn't a social call because the lights in the house were all out.

"Look, Randy. Here's what I'm going to do. I'll walk down there now, and I'll find your cigarette. It's in the middle of that small green area, right?"

He nodded, but the furrow on his forehead had returned.

"I'll find the cigarette so I can verify your story, and that will absolve you of any guilt. Well, any guilt except plain stupidity, because you know it's not smart to smoke out there around all those bushes and trees and dead grass, right?"

He nodded slowly again.

"And not to mention, it's stupid to smoke at all, right?" I think I maxed out on the lecture-o-meter about then, because he just stared at me. "So, I'm going to go look for that now, but I need you to do something for me. I need you to stay here with my dogs. I don't want to take them and have them running around a crime scene, and I most definitely don't want to leave them here alone. Will you stay here with them?"

"Yeah, sure, no worries. Your dogs and I are tight." He stood up to move to the couch, dumping several dog toys from his lap and nearly tripping over a dozen more piled at his feet. Clearly Shiner knew this kid as the human-who-throws-toys-for-me.

I got up and put out a few more cookies. I handed him the remote. "I've got HBO and there's about four ESPN channels on there. Sorry, I don't think I have any porn channels." Oops, over the top again. He looked at me like he thought I was a bit strange. I sat down again "Look, Randy, this is really important to me. I can count on you to stay here with them, right? You know, dogs would lay down their lives for us, and in return, they trust us to keep them safe. So, I can trust you, right?"

"Yes. Yes, you can, Miz Estela," he vowed solemnly. Then, with the tiniest hint of a grin, he went on, "I'll be like that elephant that sits on the nest no matter what." I patted his knee, atta-boy style. I told the dogs I'd be right back, and headed off. Didn't seem to be any point in taking anything with me, as I was only going down to look for the cigarette to confirm Randy's story. Even so, it might be good idea to take someone else along, so at the last minute I veered across the road to see if Lauren would join me.

As I climbed Valerie and Lauren's porch steps, a door slammed inside, followed by loud, angry sounds. I hesitated. The words were muffled, but more angry yelling followed and then a crash of glassware shattering. Tiptoeing away, I took a circuitous route so as not to be visible from the windows. How embarrassing!

Possibly another companion could be rounded up, but really, the whole errand would take five minutes. Slipping along the side of Will's garage, I got to the place where the rear yard was accessible without going through the crime scene tape. Like most of our houses, the area back there was brushy mixed with foxtail-type weeds. Will had taken a stab at clearing the brush away from the house a few yards. As I'd seen before, he had scattered grass seed near the rear steps and watered it in complete violation of HOA landscaping rules. Lucky for everyone, the lawn had been recently mowed. I began to search carefully. With the rain on the night of fire, the cigarette might have worked its way down into the thatch, maybe broken up a little. Still, the grass was low, so a cigarette butt should be visible. Looking up to the rock where I had been flicking my experimental butts the day before, I visually traced a likely trajectory to the grass. Barring any interference with the flight pattern, Randy's missile should have landed right about...I bent lower and pulled something light-colored from between blades of grass. Nope, it was a stick.

After several more minutes of searching, I was still coming up empty. Again, I tried to imagine Wally pouring gasoline, seeing the kids on the hillside above, throwing the can, and getting ready to run off toward home. Taking up a position about where I imagined he might have been standing, I looked around again. Nothing. I looked around the edges of the green. Nothing! I was getting frustrated. If that cigarette was there and had not been moved, I would have found it. On the other hand, there was no burned area leading from the middle of the grass to the rear of the blackened house either. If Randy's cigarette had landed where he said it landed, it may have been moved since then, but it hadn't started any fire. If it landed closer to the house than he described, the fire would have started closer to 8:00 p.m. than 9:00 p.m. Randy was off the hook, in my opinion.

Wait! Hello, what was that? A pile of dog poop at the edge of the weeds near the lawn. What was worse, it was familiar dog poop. So that was what those dogs were doing out here the night of the fire. And, that poop had been stepped in. The clear print of a smallish pointy shoe was planted right in the middle of this pile. About two feet away, another print tracked the poop in the direction of the trail headed downhill. I scanned off in the direction of Wally's.

Wally poured the gasoline just before 8:00 p.m. Someone with a small shoe size stepped in the poop on her way downhill sometime after it was deposited at 8:45 p.m. However it was accomplished, I knew Wally was responsible for those crimes. And Wally is not smart. He's evil, but he's not smart. He tried to cover his tracks, but he also left some incriminating evidence, the poop being a prime example. Climbing through the brush and connecting with the trail, I headed down canyon. Sure enough, about six feet farther along in the direction of Wally's there was another faint track of dog poop from the bottom of a smallish shoe. I got to the rock where Delia had been sitting with her gun the day before. Climbing up, I sat down for a good think. Wally's driveway was below me, and I could see his car parked facing out, blocking the drive. It certainly looked like he was planning to make a quick getaway. If someone didn't do something fast, he was going to be gone.

I slid down and walked to the point where the photographs of Wally and Sofia were taken. Wally's porch was clearly visible from here. The house was very quiet. No one was moving. The only sound was a squeak as the battered screen door blew gently out and then in again with the breeze. Watching the windows, I saw no movement inside. No smoke from the chimney. The house appeared to be deserted. I tried to remember if Wally and Tina had a second car. Maybe they had already left, and parked the other car to block the driveway, or as a decoy?

Realizing belatedly that if I could see Wally's windows clearly from my vantage point it was also likely that I could be seen, I backed carefully down behind some brush. What if I had already been spotted? I watched for a while again, but still saw no movement anywhere.

I stepped out to the main trail again and continued down toward Wally's, listening carefully, walking silently. The trail skirted around behind the house and began its descent to the creek bed. I stayed at the top and looked around for a way to get closer to the rear of Wally's house. I could see the ridge of the roof and the chimney in front of me. Then I found it. A little rabbit trail of a spur came right up out of the back edge of his yard. This must be how Wally gets on this trail without being seen, I reasoned. I got down low and crept forward. Yowch! My whole weight was on the heel of my right hand where one of those nasty goat's-head-type thorns had penetrated deep into the flesh. Great, now I'm going to get lockjaw. I succeeded in not screaming, but whimpering was inevitable. I wrapped my left sleeve around the thorn and tried to pull it out with my left hand. Yowch, again! Its smaller points stabbed my rescuing fingers while the main thorn remained deeply embedded.

I would have gotten up and run to get medical help, or some reasonable facsimile thereof, but I was trapped under the bushes, needing both hands to get out, and anyway I didn't think I could stand the pain long enough to run. I tried again to pull, and with a searing burn, finally succeeded in freeing the thorn, first from in my flesh, and then from being tangled in my sleeve. There was no blood. I put pressure on the site of the wound and rolled onto my heels, considering my next move. I didn't roll too far back, as I didn't want another of those thorns embedded anywhere else in my anatomy.

After a few minutes, I still had not seen any movement or heard any sounds around Wally's house. The downstairs had no window coverings and nothing was moving in there. The upstairs looked the same. I carefully scrutinized every window. For a second something moved behind one of those small upstairs windows, but then I realized it was only a curtain blowing slightly with the same breeze that was pushing the screen door around on the front porch. There were no lights on anywhere. No sounds of the television, no radio, no dishes clattering in the kitchen. The place looked completely abandoned.

From this angle, I could see a rusting metal garden shed, maybe ten feet square, directly in front of me. Wally's place didn't have a garage, so this shed would be where shovels and tools, fertilizer and buckets, and old broken things would be stored. This would be the place where Wally stored the can and the gas that he used to start the fire. Maybe there were more gas cans in that shed, or other evidence of Wally's crimes. It's in the news all the time about how criminals get away with their crimes, for years sometimes, only because the neighbors didn't want to be nosy. Even if suspicious, they look the other way. The more I stared at that shed, the more I knew that's where the evidence would be found. Unless Wally had taken it with him and already run.

All I had to do was get a quick look inside. If there were other gas cans in there, maybe ones that had been purchased at the same time and place as the one the deputy already had in his possession, that would be material evidence against Wally. We had witnesses who put him inside Will's house during the two-hour window when Will must have died. And the shed was not locked. I could see the door standing partly open. Unfortunately, the outside of the door faced me so I couldn't see inside. Nevertheless, all it would take would be a quick slide down the rabbit trail, and then a brisk walk, glancing inside as I passed. Then I could walk fast by Wally's car, and come out almost in Helen's front yard. Once there, someone could surely help me with this throbbing, searing, fiery ache in my hand now consuming almost my entire consciousness. Maybe Delia could help. Delia was a nurse. Or maybe DeVon could help; he probably had some kind of drugs.

The only flaw in my plan was that the arthritis in my right knee was really kicking up, and I wasn't sure I could unbend and make it work right in the crouched position. Why had I not followed my yoga regimen? Slowly uncurling both legs, I stretched them out in front of me, and then kind of slid down the embankment into Wally's yard, landing maybe ten feet behind the shed. Once at the bottom, I froze. Still no sound, no movement from the house. Gingerly, I rose and worked both knees until I knew they would hold my weight. Creeping silently past the door of the shed, I stopped at the threshold to look into the darkened interior.

Yes, I know, and I agree. Don't go in there! The thing is, as so often happens in life, I was only taking one step at a time, putting one foot in front of the other, and each decision seemed to follow naturally from the one before. Upon reflection, I should never have put myself into that situation, but at the time, each step seemed to make sense, and no step by itself seemed inherently dangerous.

That last step, unfortunately, was my big mistake. One foot across the threshold into the darkened storage shed, and it was all over. A body slammed into mine from the side and I went down, hitting my head on something hard as I went. Not unconscious, my head was ringing and pain exploded on my cheekbone. The door to the shed swung shut with a bang. I was imprisoned! The knowledge of what happened to Will streaked through my mind, and panic began rising.

I wasn't alone. Heavy breathing, the smell of something feral and full of evil, and then, coming from somewhere deep in his chest, a half growl, half chuckle, "Heh, heh, heh." Nothing more. I curled my legs under me, and, still cradling one hand in the other, rose unsteadily to stand. Enough light came in at the corners of the shed, I could see it was Wally. His face in almost complete darkness, the light caught the outer frizzes of his hair, giving him an aura of horror, like some demon angel. To go with the image, he made the sound again, "Heh, heh, heh." In a rumbling whisper he said, "I got you now, bitch." He moved closer, so close his warm breath was wet on my face. He smelled like he'd been eating mothballs. He shifted his weight, moving his body almost on top of mine. I couldn't see his hands in the darkness, but instinctively I shrank away. The back of my knees came up against a pile of junk, keeping me from going any farther. I felt, rather than saw, him reaching out to touch me. Another thought flashed about all the other women and girls Wally had abused and taken advantage of in his life. At that moment, everything shifted for me.

"Leave me alone you disgusting rat!" I bellowed. "Get away from me!" I yelled in as deep, and as loud a voice as I could muster. I knew I was not up for a physical struggle with him. He was too much bigger. A fight would end quickly, and then Wally could do whatever he wanted. I was probably too far away and inside a shed, so no one could hear my yells. Neither did I have much faith that anyone in Arroyo Loco would come running to my rescue, even if they did hear me. Although many folks here take careful note of their neighbors' comings and goings, when someone genuinely needs help, others always seem to be occupied elsewhere.

My reason for yelling was visceral, pure anger, rising out of a desire to intimidate Wally, maybe an impossible task. After all, the man had spent time in prison and had probably already killed one person. I don't know what I was thinking. "Leave me alone," I bellowed again and made a slight threatening movement toward Wally and the door. Big mistake. He swung out blindly with a curled fist and clipped me on the neck and jaw. I heard something big crack. Must have been his hand because he screamed like an injured rodent. His blow knocked me sideways. I hit my head again, and this time I tasted blood. Still squealing, Wally kicked viciously at my shins, opening up more scrapes. He fell backward, knocking the door open. The light blinded me, but it was not to reveal my salvation. "Tina!" he screamed. "Tina, get out here!" He stood leaning against the open door and breathing heavily. We both heard the tiny voice from somewhere outside, but I couldn't discern the words. "Bring me that other syringe, and bring it fast!" Wally yelled. Another faint reply. Wally stood taller and his voice lost its squealing edge, became more authoritative. "Bring it now, or I'll use it on you!"

To show I wasn't done yet, I struggled into a standing position again. When I was growing up, my cousins always told me, Stel, if you don't want to fight anymore, stay down, but I never could. I always had to prove my opponent hadn't gotten the best of me.

Wally and I stared hatefully at one another while he waited for Tina. I tried to think of a plan. The door was only open about six inches, and Wally's body filled most of that space. Using what light there was, I searched around to see if there might be something to use as a weapon. I knew he was watching me, but I figured I wasn't counting on surprise here. I only needed something big enough to do some real damage if I swung it. I wanted something that he wouldn't grab and whack me with if I missed. I didn't see much. Not even a shovel or a rake. I did see another red plastic gas can, for whatever that's worth. In fact, three of them were at my feet. They were the reason I couldn't move around, and kept losing my balance whenever Wally hit me. At least a couple of those cans were still full. Apparently, Wally had more fiery ideas.

As if reading my thoughts, he chuckled evilly. The afternoon sunlight revealed dark gaps where he was missing side teeth, and his big front teeth were yellowed like a rat's. His foul grin grew wider. "I'm gonna jab you with this needle, then set fire to this whole place, bitch. You're gonna burn alive, Estela Nogales, like the witch you are." Again with the, "Heh, heh, heh."

He scowled and turned his eyes toward the house. I considered rushing him, but I couldn't make myself move closer. What if Tina really did have a tranquilizer powerful enough to knock me out and some way to get it in me while I was trying to fight Wally off?

"Tina! Hurry up! What's taking so long? Get out here!" He turned to me again. He whispered hoarsely, "I was gonna use this on her, then burn up my own place. Leave her here." He looked off at the tree tops for a minute, almost wistful. "Too bad I didn't tell her to bring more of this stuff home. Then I could do you both." Again with the half-toothless leer. "This barbiturate stuff is good. One jab and boom—a big old guy like Will goes down, and all the fight goes out. Then you can kill him any way you want." Wally turned and lifted his lip over his pointy yellow front teeth. "Or do anything to you I want.

"That old buzzard Will shoulda minded his own business," Wally spat at me, now glaring almost through me. "What you people shoulda got is that I am not going back to prison. If you'da left me alone, nobody would'a got hurt. I saw you watching me sometimes, and those other old biddies. It's like Sunshine said, I just like to play with the little girls. I don't hurt nobody." The grin again, followed quickly by another angry glare. "But no, you haf'ta keep talking me down, watching me, then him sneaking around taking his pictures and torturing me with those damn things. I am not going back to prison, bitch, and nobody's gonna make me. So now you're dead too, from not minding your own business." He stopped talking and his eyes narrowed, "Anyhow, those damn photographs are gone. All'a Will's pictures got burned up."

And now Wally was about to kill the one remaining person who might put all of those pieces together. Belatedly, I realized he must have seen me coming down the trail earlier and was lying in wait for me inside the shed. He probably figured he could hit me on the head, knock me unconscious, and then burn the shed down along with Tina and the house. He likely wouldn't get away with a second and third murder and arson fire, but maybe he hoped to have time to be far away and well-hidden before law enforcement came after him. Like I said, Wally is evil, but he's not the brightest bulb.

Finally, an idea sparked, at least something I could try. I might not have a shovel, or even an old piece of board, but I wasn't helpless. Leaning down, I picked up one of the full gas cans, holding it in front of me.

"Bitch. You're gonna die," Wally snarled. Eww! He got spit on me! Now I was really mad. Suddenly, Tina was there. Wally grabbed something from her, put it to his mouth, and spat the protective cap of a syringe into the dirt. Holding the syringe curled in his fist, he let go of the door and stepped menacingly forward, raising his hand to stab me.

Instead of backing up, I rushed him using the heavy plastic gas can as a combination battering ram and shield. It was a calculated risk, as I still had plenty of exposed body parts into which Wally could embed the flying needle. My most effective weapon was my voice. In the loudest bellow I could bring from the deepest part of my chest, I hollered again, "Get away from me, Wally! Get away from me!" We crashed into one another, him pushing against the can with one hand and trying to stab me with the other. He was much stronger, and I fell backward again.

We both heard them at exactly the same moment. Happy voices of women coming down the trail from behind the house. In a singsong, Freda cried out, "Ooh, look at me! I'm hiking through the woods! Tra-la!" Then she broke into song, "Val-de-rah, val-de-ree, val-de-rah-ha-ha!"

"Pipe down, Freda." That was Helen. "We're supposed to be searching for Estela. I think I heard something."

Wally froze, and I yelled again, "Get away from me, Wally!" There was a fraction of a second when I feared they would go on down the trail and bypass Wally's house completely. Then Nina said, "There! I heard it too. There's his house, right there! Estela's down there! Now, how do we get there?" There was a chorus of, "Estela, we're coming!" Then the sound of large animals crashing through underbrush, a sliding sound and an "Oomph!" as though someone had taken the fast track to the bottom of the embankment.

If Wally intended to drug me, set the shed on fire, and escape, he clearly had no time left to execute his plan. I knew that, and in the next fraction of a second, he knew it too. He took another ineffectual swipe in my direction with the syringe, threw it at me, then turned and ran. I scrambled to the door of the shed, where I watched him flee.

His shoes flopped and his baggy pants drooped around his hips as he ran clumsily toward the car, pulled open the driver's door, and crammed himself inside. The car was already rolling when Tina banged out the screen door and flew off the porch, running after him barefoot.

"Wally! Wally, honey, wait for me!" she cried. In spite of the sharp gravel, she continued to limp after him, but he didn't hesitate. As she reached the rear of the car, he gunned the engine and shot down the drive, throwing gravel and dirt into her face. The car turned and disappeared down canyon. Tina stood there for a moment, wiping her mouth and eyes with the ragged sleeve of her over-sized sweater, sobbing, "Wally?" She turned and returned slowly to the porch. Throwing herself down on the top step, she buried her face in her hands, whimpering.

I felt an arm around me and turned to find Lauren there, along with Nina, Helen, and Freda. They had come to rescue me. Fresh scratches bled on Helen's face. Nina stooped to wipe some dust from her matte-finish fine-leather Gucci loafers.

"Hola, Chica!" she said as she smoothed hair away from her face. Lauren stood in silence with her arm wrapped tightly around my shoulder. She seemed to be trembling slightly, but maybe that was me.

Guess I must have been more scared than I realized because for a few minutes all I could do was hug my friends and sigh my relief. "Wow. Oh, wow. You guys showed up just in time." After a few seconds, I asked, "How on earth did you know to come? How did you find me?"

"Oh," Freda said, "Randy called me. He said go find you. He said you must be in trouble because you didn't come home. He said to look in Will's yard, then go to Wally's. Trouble, always it comes back to Wally, he said. So here we've come!" She smiled brightly, the sunshine glinting in her impossibly orange-red hair.

Mopping a trickle of blood off her cheek, Helen added, "Freda called Nina, then Nina beeped me when she drove by, and Lauren rushed out when we parked out front of her place." She looked around, "We all came rushing out."

"So, here we all are again," I said, not ready yet to laugh.

"Yes, and it's a good thing you told us about this trail," added Nina. "If we had gone all the way out to the road and come up that driveway," she pointed, "it would have taken us much longer."

We looked out where Wally's car had disappeared. "Plus, by now we would all be roadkill," Helen added somberly. "Wally would have happily flattened every one of us."

I thought about how each person in Arroyo Loco contributed toward building community or destroying it. One builds community by helping others and trusting, while another tears community apart by taking advantage of that trust and using others. Wally's crimes were made possible by the rest of us wanting to trust and look at the positive. At the same time, he had now created a climate of fear and suspicion among us that would make it harder to live in community. Will seemed to derive pleasure from tormenting and annoying others. Living in a place where most of the rest of us were trying to live in peace gave him ample opportunity to find victims. Amanita liked to make other people march to her rules, and Arroyo Loco gave her a set of captive marchers. Betsy needed an audience and constant attention, and we provided it.

On the bright side, it seemed I had friends here after all, friends who had organized and come to look for me. I felt safe standing there with them. Although I knew I would not soon forget Wally's leering face coming at me out of the darkness in that smelly shed, I was also surrounded now by the smiles of my friends.

Still huddled in a heap, Tina whimpered. There she sat, a wife without her husband. After everything she had done to support him, now she sat alone and abandoned. It isn't supposed to be like that, but we all know how easily and often that train comes off its tracks. As if she could sense my stare, she lifted her head, stringy black hair obscuring her expression. "He made me do it," she whimpered. What we could see of her face was red, her eyes almost swollen shut. She looked like she'd been crying for days. "He made me do it," she wailed again. "Look! See?" She held an arm and hand out, but all I could see was the dirty sweater. "I burned my hand. He gave me matches and told me to go light the fire." She buried her face in her lap again. "I burned my hand." Bearing witness to her story, a pair of small shoes sat on the stoop, smeared with the remains of the dog poop deposited in Will's backyard.

CHAPTER TWELVE

The five of us shifted awkwardly and looked at each other. Normally we might go comfort her, but no one moved in Tina's direction. Like everyone's mom, mine used to say, "You made your bed. Now you have to lie in it." Maybe there are ways to explain away Tina's behavior. From what little I knew, she and Wally had a typical marriage in which loyalty to the partner plays a central role. In sickness and in health, until death do you part and so on. Does that vow absolve each partner of individual responsibility to the wider community? In our legal system it does, married partners cannot be compelled to testify against one another in court. Does Tina's emotional dependence on Wally decrease her culpability in these crimes? Psychologists use a diagnostic category called Dependent Personality Disorder, classifying behavior like Tina's as a form of mental illness. That diagnosis can be, and in Tina's case, probably would be, used as a defense against criminal charges.

Tina wailed again, "Wally, Wally, come back for me!" She looked at us beseechingly, a completely bereft, dirty bundle on the old wooden porch step. An exclusive relationship with one other person makes for a very thin safety net. Each of my friends with me that day served as testament to the need for a larger network of mutual support in all our lives. I looked around at them, overwhelmed with appreciation for their presence. As she huddled on the porch right now, Tina was a poster child for the need to maintain that larger network of support even when also involved in a partnership.

"Come on," I said quietly to my friends. "Let's go to my house and tell Randy everything's okay. We can call the deputy sheriff from there."

I went back to the shed. We were not going to go searching around in there for the broken and heavily finger-printed syringe, but there was no sense leaving the shed open for someone else to rummage around. I flipped the hasp and snapped the padlock closed. Then I wrapped each arm around a friend. As we passed the end of the porch I caught Helen's eye and shot a glance over to Tina. We all stopped as Helen put a hand on Tina's shoulder.

"Come on Tina," she said. "You're coming with us." With dirty tracks of tears still staining her reddened face, Tina looked up at Helen, a glimmer of hope in her eyes. My stomach gave another of those visceral lurches. Tina was not being invited to come along with us out of friendship. She had admitted to lighting the fire that could have done much more damage in our canyon. If Will was still alive when that fire started, Tina had also killed him. She was being invited to come along so we could make sure she faced the sad end that her behavior had earned her.

It was a cinch we weren't going back up that embankment to take the shortcut trail, so the six of us trooped together down the driveway. As we reached the road, the cavalry was arriving in the form of Dick, pompous as ever, followed closely by Ernie, trying to elbow Dick out of the lead. Dick carried a long shotgun, a museum piece that looked like he'd taken it off its display above his fireplace. He would likely have injured himself badly if he tried to fire that old thing. Ernie was no less threatening, wielding a long-handled axe borrowed from the fire engine. From uphill, Bryce came dashing down to us in bedroom slippers, carrying a junior-sized baseball bat.

Clearing his throat to achieve the deepest rumble possible, Dick demanded, "What's going on here? Bryce called and said you girls were all hanging around behind Will's. That is a crime scene, you know."

"Yeah," echoed Bryce. "It's a crime scene. You're really gonna catch it now." Happily, Ernie decided there was such a thing as enough pomposity, and he stepped back, joining Raymond who was only now walking up.

There was a half-second pause. Then I jumped in, "Well, you know, Dick," I took in the rest of the crowd in a glance, "I think I'll tell the whole story to the sheriff in the morning, and maybe at a meeting where I can tell everyone at once. Cut down on the rumors and misinformation, you know? For now I've got to get home." Dick glared at me from under his bushy, greying eyebrows, but fortunately there was nothing he could do to make me talk.

I looked behind me. "Oh, yeah. You can take custody of Tina here, and call Deputy Muñoz. Tina confessed in front of five witnesses to setting fire to Will's while Wally was down at the roadhouse."

This earned a collective gasp from the four men. Helen pushed Tina gently forward. Placated, Dick and Ernie took Tina under their command. Each one grabbed an arm and they turned to hustle her away. They made it about fifteen feet before a loud argument erupted about where they were taking her. Trailing along behind them, Bryce had his own opinion.

"Oh, Bryce," I called. "There are a pair of shoes on Wally's front deck. Those are important evidence. You should go guard those until the deputy can get here. Don't let anyone touch them. Bryce looked from me to the rapidly retreating party escorting Tina, and back. Then he trotted off down Wally's driveway in the direction of the porch. Thank goodness, that was the last I saw of him for several days.

Sunshine and Betsy were rushing toward the group as we turned to go, but they had missed the action. For once, Betsy hadn't been sneaking around behind me. Raymond seemed relieved, and I think he was smiling as he wrapped an affectionate arm around Sunshine and they headed off together. The last I saw of Betsy, she was jumping up and down next to Dick trying to get a word in edgewise and demanding to know what had happened. Maybe Betsy so often feels not heard because she's so darn short and is thus easily and literally overlooked.

The rest of us went on up the hill. As we neared Lauren's house, she cut a guilty look that way. Valerie stood in the shadows of the porch overhang, her eyes narrowed and her arms crossed angrily. "Guess I'd better go," Lauren mumbled, and she slunk home.

Nina, Freda, Helen, and I piled in through my kitchen door. Randy was stretched out on the couch, sound asleep, snoring loudly, with the Cal/Stanford game on full volume. So much for his worrying about me. Shiner had sprawled out on top of Randy, all four legs in the air and his head nestled under Randy's chin. Shiner jumped down, scattering a half-dozen abandoned dog toys, poking Randy hard in the gut with a sharp elbow, and waking him up. For future reference, and I speak from experience, although they often want to be quite cuddly, border collies do not usually make good lap dogs.

After a second, Scout too strolled out from somewhere down the hall, stretched and came forward for a welcoming pat. Sleeping on my bed again, no doubt. Yep, everyone here at home had really been worrying about me. I let the dogs outside and dragged Randy out with us. As he scratched his belly and woke up, I quickly explained that he was not in trouble—this time. His cigarette had not ignited anything. He and his friends would need to testify when Wally was caught and brought to trial. And they would need to stop smoking in that explosive canyon. For good measure, I added my appreciation for their watchfulness over our community from their vantage along the trail, but requested him to please stop rifling through my pantry and helping himself to other people's belongings. He nodded solemnly, or maybe sleepily. Then I told him to go home and gently pushed him out the screen door.

"Oh, wait. Randy?" He stopped and looked at me. "People were talking this morning about ice cream disappearing from the freezer in the roadhouse. Did you kids have anything to do with taking that ice cream?"

"Naw," he assured me. "If it was liquor we mighta, but not ice cream." Then grinning enigmatically, he added, "But I do know who is sneakin' down there and eating it, and it's not who you think it is." With that, he was gone. Yet another unsolved mystery in Arroyo Loco.

I had tried to make this conversation quick so I could get inside and play hostess, but it was already too late when I got there. The football game was off, Helen and Freda were figuring out my cantankerous old coffeemaker, and someone had dug half a cheesecake out of the freezer. I hoped it was still edible. Luckily, I keep a stockpile of homemade cookies in there too. Nina gathered chairs around the dining table while Helen dug up mugs, plates, and forks. Freda poured coffee. Still babying my injured hand, I rolled my desk chair in from the office. The four of us settled down.

"Now, Estela," Nina gushed, "spill! What happened with Wally? You must have really done something to him, as fast as he took off when we got there!"

"Hoo-whee," Helen laughed, "Wally the Clown breaks the six-minute mile!"

"It wasn't me." After a second, I joined in the laughter. It was going to be hard for me to think of Wally as something as harmless as a clown after I'd seen that evil grin of his. "It was you guys getting there. All you middle-aged ladies sliding down through the underbrush and suddenly appearing in his yard—that's what scared the pants off him."

"Yes, really, it very nearly did scare the pants off him," Nina smiled. "I thought he might not make it to the car. Wonder if he wears them like that so he can get them off in a hurry, you know, when.... " She gazed quizzically at a corner of the ceiling.

"Eeww!" we joined in a chorus.

"No, really," I laughed. "It was you guys showing up when you did. You rescued me."

"Oh, nonsense," Nina waved her hand dismissively. "All we did was fall down the hill." How true it is that friends do rescue us, and not usually through some valiant act of heroism either. Usually by being there with us when we need them.

"Anyway, tell us everything that happened, Estela. Don't leave anything out!" Nina insisted.

I quickly outlined the events leading to my presence in the storage shed. I told them about Wally's attack on me and the threats he made. "Wally told me he injected Will with barbiturates, like what a veterinarian uses to euthanize animals, and was planning to do the same to Tina," I added. Then, to get it clear in my own mind, I ran through the probable timeline of Will's murder. "We know he was alive at six because DeVon almost ran him down in the driveway and Lauren saw him then." Everyone nodded.

"Then somewhere between seven and eight o'clock Wally was inside the house with Will, and we have witnesses who saw Wally come out of the house no later than eight. Wally knew Will had seen him with Sofia and had those photographs."

"Maybe Wally was looking for the photographs?" Freda speculated.

"That's probably true," I agreed. "I don't think Wally ever heard about the photographs stuffed into Sunshine's mailbox. That's probably why he didn't leave town. He assumed the photographs were in the house when it burned down, so no one would suspect him. Either he saw those photographs when he injected Will, or he looked and couldn't find them. Maybe he left them on the bed with Will. In any case, he poured gasoline around thinking the fire would destroy the evidence and kill the only witness."

"Oh, my," Freda sighed thoughtfully. "Then sometime between the time Wally poured the gasoline and the time the house burned down, the photographs were moved from inside the house to Sunshine's mailbox."

"Yes," agreed Nina. "It had to be Janet. She must have found the photographs lying next to Will. She wanted someone else to know what Wally did. It makes sense that she would entrust them to Sunshine, too, since Sunshine helped her get out of Arroyo Loco and away from Will."

"Well, maybe Wally couldn't find the photographs. Maybe that's why he burned the whole house down," Helen suggested.

I nodded solemnly, then had second thoughts. "Wait, Wally had already bought the gasoline by then, right?"

"Okay, you have a point there. So the arson was planned in advance," Helen concluded.

"The murder was planned in advance too," I ventured. "Wally had two syringes of barbiturates, and he used one on Will." The table grew very quiet. "Wally must have drugged Will and laid him out on the bed as though he was dead. He put the photographs next to Will, then went home, got his can of gasoline, and poured it around the rear of the house. Randy and his friends saw him doing that. Wally went off for his usual Friday night drink with Ernie and Thomas. He was going slightly later than his usual time, so he probably went by way of the trail. Not too many people would see him that way."

"Yes, I think so too," agreed Nina. "I was working right in front in my dining room, and I didn't see him go by."

"Shortly after Wally left, Janet and Kenneth arrived." I continued, "They got Janet's things, found Will in bed, asleep, or dead, or close to it, said their goodbyes, and left. They stopped briefly to talk to Graciela. Oh, and Janet took the photographs and stuffed them into Sunshine's mailbox."

Helen picked up the timeline, "Sometime after Wally got to the roadhouse, Tina went up to Will's and lit the fire."

"Yeah," I nodded. "Maybe right before nine or so, after Janet left, and the dogs and I walked past."

"Then, by the time I saw it was after nine, quite a bit burning by then, yes?" Freda confirmed.

I was puzzled. "There's one piece I still don't get...."

"Well, here's the piece I still don't get," Helen interrupted. "Who cut the wire on my cat cage? And why? Why would someone do that?" Our attention shifted to Helen. How can some people change direction so fast? Or maybe it was me. Helen had probably never stopped thinking about her cats.

"Oh, well, Wally was trying to distract everyone, yes, don't you think?" Freda asked.

"Hmm," I said. "Seems like Wally's been laying low since the fire. I don't think he would have risked coming out for petty vandalism. Not that harming your cats was in any way petty," I hastily added.

"Yes," Nina said. "Who cut that cage and why will remain one more mystery for the time being. One thing we do know is, for once it wasn't Will!"

"That's what I was going to ask," I tried again. "When, exactly did Will die? Was he still alive, only unconscious when Janet and Kenneth were there...or not? If he was still alive, who killed him? Wally, or Janet, or Tina? Or who?"

Nina stared. "Do you mean Wally told Tina to go light that fire, knowing Will would die in it? He intentionally caused Tina to murder Will?" She shook her head slowly. Hard to believe anyone could be that evil.

I said something about how the coroner would have to determine if Will was still breathing when the fire started, then Helen broke in.

"Tina cooked him. It had to be Tina. If all Wally gave him was a veterinarian dose of barbiturates, he would have only been sleeping when the fire started. What I don't get is why Tina would do it. Why didn't she leave him? She could take care of herself. She's the one who works. She's not financially dependent."

"Maybe something like that Stockholm Syndrome," Freda suggested. "You know, the captive joins in with the captor."

"Okay, what do you think, Stel? You're the expert on this psychological stuff," Helen asked, genuinely puzzled.

"Yeah, well, it's like Freda suggested. The captor, in this case the wife, doesn't trust her own instincts any longer. The manipulation exerted by the husband is so deep, and has gone on for so long, she's really under his control. He has her convinced he's only trying to protect her from the outside world and that he's the only person who really cares about her. Probably even he believes that. But the reality is, it's all about power. He's trying to control her, to keep her from leaving him. At the beginning, he's not such a bad guy. He's only insecure that she'll leave him. Once he has established control, knows she can't or won't leave him for whatever reason, that is when he becomes abusive. By then she thinks she has no option but to stay with him and do whatever he wants."

"Yes, Helen. There are other ways than financial to be dependent on a man," Nina added quietly, looking down at the table.

With a confused scowl, Helen said, "But...."

"No, wait, Helen. I know because I was there once, you know, with my husband, Enzo," Nina said. She took a deep breath. "Enzo di Rossi. It all started like a wonderful romantic movie. He swept me off my feet. From the minute we first met, he was always there. He took me out to beautiful places, showered me with affection. It was exactly like I'd always dreamed it would be. He only wanted to be with me, and wanted me to only be with him. When we got married, we eloped by ourselves to Reno.

"My mother and family were heartbroken to not have a big white wedding with all the family there, but Enzo said he didn't want to share me with anyone. He told me I would never have to work. He found a great job in Texas, so we moved away from all of my family and friends. He said it was better because we always got into a fight after I saw anyone in my family. Which was true, we did, but only because he started it. He told me my mother said ugly things about me. I was such a fool, I believed him. I even made up stories about how badly my family had treated me, so he could tell me again how he was the only one who ever really loved me. It was me and him against the rest of the world. When Angela was born, he wouldn't let anyone in my family come to visit until she was several months old. He said we needed time to bond. Broke my mother's heart. Eventually, it was easier to stay disconnected, so I told my family I didn't want to see them any longer. By then, I was believing my own stories. The abuse started with sniping little remarks. Enzo would tear me down verbally, tell me I had to depend on him because I would never be able to get a job, or keep one. Tell me I was stupid, lazy, overreacting, not a good mother. He would drink too much. But there I was. What could I do? Where could I go? I had cut off all my ties. I had no one to turn to for support. Later, he'd say he was sorry and that he wouldn't do it again, and then he did. Gradually it got worse.

"I stayed with him until Angela was thirteen. Enzo started yelling at her, trying to control her too, cutting her down. I let it happen to me, but when it started happening to her, I knew we had to leave. I was so scared. He said he'd kill me, or himself, if I left. He chased us for months and threatened to kill me if I didn't go back. He was serious too. I don't know how, but he found out where we were staying in a crummy motel in Turlock and came after us. He ran a red light. The accident killed him and two innocent people in the other car. I feel so guilty. If I had stayed with him, they would still be alive."

"Oh, Nina, I'm so sorry," I managed, as everyone else murmured similar sentiments. "Do you ever see your family now?"

"No," she sighed. "I've let them down so often and been so cruel to them, I can't bear to try. Even today, I still sort of believe some of those ugly things I used to say about them. Every once in a while my sister sends a short email. Someone's getting married. Someone else has a baby, you know. That kind of thing." She looked around at us. We were all giving her the sad-puppy eyes. "The hardest part is, now that Angela is out of college and off on her own, she doesn't want to have much to do with me. She never knew what it was like to have a close extended family, and she knows I deprived her of that by cutting us off from my family. So now I don't even have her. I am alone." Nina looked around the table and gave us all a smile that never reached her eyes. "Except for my friends, of course." With a deep breath, she pulled herself up to perfect posture and let her social façade drape back into place.

"Well, I guess you're right. Something like that probably happened to Tina," Helen concluded. "Remember when Wally called her his "tiny China doll," and I about lost my lunch?" She got a few weak smiles for that. "I wonder," Helen continued, "do you think Tina was a mail-order bride? I mean like from China, literally? Who else would marry that creep? I think he must be brain-damaged."

"Hmm," I shook my head. "You do have to wonder, where is Tina's family? She doesn't have any friends that I know about."

"I guess a lot of people don't have connections, for a lot of reasons," Helen added quietly.

That was certainly true. We'd all heard Nina's sad tale. Looking around the table, I wondered about Helen's story. I had never heard her mention children or siblings. She did tell me once she always wanted to be a "Mrs. Somebody," and had been engaged a couple of times. Sadly she'd never been able to, as she'd put it, "close the deal." So she did not have a former husband or partner. And what about Freda? Was she really descended from an Austrian aristocrat? I knew there was a son somewhere, but I'd never met him, or seen him visit. Then there were Lauren and Valerie. They seemed to be sort of an island unto themselves too. How could we all live and sleep and eat so closely together and not know such simple and basic facts about one another? I made a mental note to invite them all to dinner soon. And to send cousin Diego a nice message this very evening, maybe with some money enclosed.

"You know," Helen mused, "that thing you said about men like Wally wanting to feel more powerful than their victims? Is that why Wally gave Will that drug, the one that made him helpless?" We nodded sadly. Then I thought again about what might have happened if he had gotten that needle into me, and my friends had not come along. I shuddered, a chill running all the way down my spine. One lonely tear finally spilled, which I quickly wiped away. I was afraid if I started, I wouldn't be able to stop.

About that time, my phone rang, announcing a call from the Carpers. Somebody grabbed it, passed it to me, and everyone quieted to listen.

It was Dick calling to tell us that the deputy sheriff had picked up Wally, speeding on the highway out of town. Apparently Muñoz wasn't as dull as I'd feared. He suspected Wally of some sort of wrongdoing early on, or maybe it was Wally's felony record that clued the deputy in to watch him. In any case, Muñoz was more or less lying in wait and stopped Wally shortly after he sped away from Arroyo Loco. Wally was being booked and giving up Tina all over the place. The deputy would be out shortly to pick up Tina. According to Dick, Tina was giving up Wally too, so they were digging one another's graves.

During the phone conversation, I held my left hand in my right, babying it where the thorn had penetrated the heel of my hand. As I hung up, I inspected the wound. Suddenly, Nina's eyes got big, staring at my hand.

"Estela, did Wally inject you too?" she cried out.

Everyone was looking at my hand now. Even as I said no, and explained about the thorn, I could feel the pain in my hand, hot and hard, with a deep puncture visible. Still not much bleeding. I'm not sure, but I think that's a bad sign.

"We need to wash that out and get ice on that immediately," Freda quickly rose and went to the freezer. "Helen, get us a small towel. Also, see if you can find some bacteria ointment and the aspirin or something." She was hacking efficiently away at my ice bin with a kitchen knife, freeing up a few cubes, while ordering others around. "Nina, look in the phonebook. We need to get her a tetanus shot right away. Right now!"

"It's Sunday afternoon," Nina protested. "Where can we get a tetanus shot now?"

"There's that doc-in-a-box on Bay Street on the right side coming into Morro Bay," Helen called as she returned with a washcloth and two small bottles from my medicine cabinet. As comforting as it was to know these people could snap into action in an emergency, I was feeling sort of left out here. I hoped Helen hadn't found anything embarrassing in that medicine cabinet.

"Yes. Yes, here it is," Nina pointed at the number in the book while dialing the phone.

"Come here, Estela, dear, and let me wash that with warm water and soap," commanded Freda. "Hurry now, here." She pulled my hand under the warm running water in the sink.

"I'll get my car." Helen called, slamming out the kitchen door.

In a very professional manner, Freda wrapped the ice in the washcloth, applied it to my wound, and then wrapped a dishtowel around the whole arrangement, making a tidy bundle. "So, Freda," I ventured, "do you have medical training? Seems like you know what you're doing here."

She raised her eyebrows quickly and gave me a fast eye roll, but all she said was, "Hmm."

"Or is that a mystery also?" I persisted.

"Oh, yes. I am a very mysterious woman," she said and gave me another enigmatic smile as she tightened the wrapping.

By the time we got the dogs secured inside, fed and watered, Helen had returned with her car. I tried insisting that, although I would probably faint when I got it, not everyone needed to accompany me for a tetanus shot, but by then we had decided to go on to the Crab Shack Cafe afterward for dinner. So we all managed to squeeze into seat belts in Helen's Honda Civic hybrid. Who would have imagined such a giant person would drive such a tiny car? Off we went.

We slowed at Wally's driveway, looking down it as far as we could see. Thank goodness my dogs had not been with me for the confrontation with Wally. There's a huge difference between putting myself in danger and putting my dogs in danger. They totally trust me to keep them safe, and I always try to be worthy of that trust. And thank goodness too for my friends. I squeezed Nina's hand with my one good one.

Community is sometimes not what we expect it to be, and it cannot be forced into being out of intentional acts or physical structures. Community is built in the same mysterious way that other social relationships are built, out of friendship and acts of kindness, out of respect, generosity of spirit, and trust. Maybe with Wally gone, and Will, who had never really been more than a pain in the neck, Arroyo Loco would have the chance to become a real community and not only a place to live.

Dear Reader,

Thank you for reading *Fire at Will's*. I hope you enjoyed it! Please take a moment and post a few words about the book on Amazon.com. Book shoppers will appreciate your thoughts, as will I.

To keep up on the news about Arroyo Loco, learn about other books in the Estela Nogales series, and contact me with comments and questions, please check out and subscribe to my web page at cherieoboyle.com. I would love to hear from you.

Thank you again for your support!

Cherie

Praise for **Iced Tee**

Iced Tee. Winner of the 2015 "Best Small Town Cozy" Mystery & Mayhem Award from Chanticleer Book Reviews.

"The second Estela Nogales mystery is more gripping than the first...Plenty of humor and a plot that will keep you guessing."

Anara Guard, author of *Remedies for Hunger*

Praise for **Missing Mom**

"This is a great "Where is she?" story about one of the residents of Arroyo Loco, which is a place I love to visit. Can't wait for the next book in the Estela Nogales series."

Pamela Beason, best-selling author of *The Only Witness*

I enjoyed *Missing Mom* the best out of the Estela Nogales Mystery Series...engaging, quirky and great summer reading!

Carole Chancellor, mystery reader

Made in the USA
Columbia, SC
01 August 2018